purge

Sarah Darer Littman

SCHOLASTIC INC.
New York Toronto London Auckland
Sydney Mexico City New Delhi Hong Kong

This book was originally published in hardcover by Scholastic Press in 2009.

ISBN 978-0-545-05237-5

12 11 10 9 8 7 6 5 4 3 2 1   10 11 12 13 14 15/0

Printed in the U.S.A.   40

First Scholastic paperback printing, April 2010

The text type was set in Gotham.
Book design by Becky Terhune

To Nancy Head Thode, for helping me find my
words and learn to use them

PROLOGUE

The bathroom might be an unusual place to have stage fright, but it's where I am and what I've got. I really need to go, and have ever since breakfast. I served my post-meal thirty-minute sentence, and now I'm sitting here trying to do what I've got to do, but Nurse Rose is outside the door, which she told me I have to keep open a crack, and I've got stage fright, because she's listening to every noise I make.

It's completely mortifying, but having a watchdog outside the bathroom door is one of the many oppressive rules they have here at Golden Slopes. There are rules for everything: the *No shoelaces in case you hang yourself* Rule, the Thirty-Minute Rule, the No Napkin in the Lap Rule, and the *Finish every single thing on your plate even if you are full or else you drink a can of Ensure* Rule. But the worst part is this: trying to do your business with someone outside the bathroom door listening.

At least she can't hear my thoughts. But if she could, this is what she'd hear echoing in my brain: *How the hell did I end up in this place?*

CHAPTER ONE

July 20th

At least they've given me a journal, even if it's just a cheapo notebook like everyone else's. Sometimes I feel like a journal is the one place I can be honest and real, where I don't have to weigh my words and worry about what I'm supposed to say and what everyone is going to think and who I'm supposed to be. On paper, I don't have to smile and pretend I'm fine even though inside I feel like I'm breaking into a thousand tiny fragments too small ever to be put together again.

But enough of all that. If I'm going to have to write a spill-it-all exposé of my life for a bunch of strangers, I guess I should start off by introducing myself.

Greetings, doctors, nurses, therapists, and other interested parties. My name is Jane Louise Ryman, but I prefer Janie. Jane seems too, well, boring, for a person like me — or rather the person I'd like to be, even if I'm not quite there yet.

I'm my mother's oldest child and my father's middle child, if that makes any sense. Dad was married to someone else before he met Mom, and he had my stepsister, the eternally can-do-no-wrong Jenny, who is twelve years older than me. Then he and Jenny's mom, Clarissa, got divorced, Dad married Mom, and they had me and then my younger brother, Harry, who's twelve, four years younger than me. So depending on how you look at it, I'm the overachieving, anxious eldest child or the mixed-up, rebellious middle one. Talk about a lose-lose situation.

My dad, Harold, or "Hal," as everyone calls him, is a hedge fund manager, which basically means he takes big sums of money from really loaded people and makes it into even bigger sums of money — or not, depending on the year. We know it's been a good year if Mom gets diamond jewelry for her birthday or we get to go to the Caribbean AND Europe in the same year. If it's been a bad year, we're lucky if we get to go to Florida to visit my grandparents.

Carole, my mom, used to work at Bayview Partners, Dad's firm. She gave it up when she had me and now she's just an upscale suburban übermom.

Perfect Jenny, Harry, Ringo, the golden retriever, and a never-ending procession of hamsters, all named Horatio, round out our *picture-perfect suburban family. Picture-perfect except for me, that is. . . .*

The funny thing is I've always hated puking. You probably think that's a strange thing to hear from someone who stands in front of a toilet and sticks her finger down her throat five or six times a day. But it's true.

When I was a kid, I always used to cry every time I threw up. It hurt my throat. It hurt my stomach. It smelled bad. I felt gross. Those 24-hour stomach flus were the worst.

If I cried every time I threw up now, we'd all drown.

What I don't understand is this: How did something I hate so much end up controlling every moment of my life?

"Time for lunch," barks Joe, the beefy male nurse with a crew cut. I think he used to be in the Marines or something — probably a drill sergeant. I can just see the guy terrorizing poor innocent recruits on their first day of basic training.

I close my new journal and follow him back into the building, which seems even more gloomy than usual except for the Technicolor spots that dance before my eyes as they adjust to the darkness after being in the bright sunshine of the smokers' courtyard.

My stomach growls. I'm here at Camp Golden Slopes because after the Incident at Perfect Jenny's Wedding, everyone decided I was bulimic, so there are a bunch of other girls here like me. Well, not completely like me, because they're *really* screwed up and I'm only *partially* screwed up. They're only like me in the eating disorder sense. We Bulimia Babes are always first to the table, because we have this strange relationship with food. We want to eat it badly, but afterward we want to puke it up equally as badly.

The anorexics are another story. They'll do anything to *avoid* eating, including hiding out at mealtimes, because they have a hate-hate relationship with food. It ends up causing plenty of friction between the bulimics and the anorexics, because we'll be sitting at the table ravenous, even for the gross Golden Slopes food, but we're not allowed to start until every one of the eating disorder patients is present and whichever nurse is head of the Eating Police for that meal tells us we can begin. It ends up being like a gang war, except instead of the Sharks and the Jets or the Bloods and the Crips, it's the Barfers and the Starvers.

Callie and Melissa, the other Barfers, are already at the table with their trays in front of them. Nurse Joe hands me my tray from the cart and I go sit down next to Callie. The entire Barfer contingent is present and accounted for, and there's not a Starver in sight.

"This sucks," says Missy, drumming her ring-laden fingers on the table. "Everything's going to be cold by the time they round up the stick insects."

She can't stand the anorexics. Missy thinks they look down their nose at her because she's — let's be blunt — overweight. It doesn't matter to them that she's got long honey-blond hair and Caribbean-blue eyes, and radiates energy like a nuclear reactor. If you ignore the extra seventy-something pounds, Missy could be on the cover of the *Sports Illustrated* Swimsuit Issue, or modeling underwear in the Victoria's Secret catalog, being lusted after by all of our brothers and dads. (You didn't seriously think your dad signed up for the Victoria's Secret catalog just so he could buy a present for your *mother*, did you?)

"Yo!" Callie shouts out to GI Joe, who is standing at the door of the dayroom watching out for incoming Starvers. "We're hungry here. Can't we go ahead and eat?"

"You know the rules, Callie," Nurse Joe replies, unmoved. "Anyway, here comes Nurse Kay with a few of our delinquent diners."

Sure enough, Nurse Kay, one of the cooler counselors at Camp Golden Slopes, enters the room, herding four Starvers before her.

"Four down, one to go," she tells Joe. "How about you go hunt for Helen this time?"

"Yeah, yeah, okay," grumbles Joe as he heads down the hallway. We can hear him calling out Helen's name, like *that's* going to get her to come out from wherever she's hiding.

Helen is the Starver-in-Chief. She has avoiding mealtimes down to an art. One day Nurse Kay found her hiding in the laundry cart, with all the dirty linens and towels. I mean you have to be pretty messed up if you're willing to bury yourself in other people's dirty sheets just so you don't have to eat.

Missy's getting seriously antsy now.

"C'mon, Nurse Kay! I'm *starving*. Why do we have to wait for Her Royal Twigness?"

Nurse Kay gives Missy her *I'm disappointed in you* look. It's effective if you're the kind of person who doesn't like to disappoint people, but from what I've learned about Missy so far, that's not something she's all that concerned with.

"Melissa, you need to learn to support your fellow patients, not insult them," says Nurse Kay. "Anyway, I'm sure Helen will be here any minute."

Sure enough, in shuffles the Queen of Lean. She's followed by Joe, who uses his broad, muscular body to block her avenue of escape.

"About frickin' time," remarks Callie.

Helen ignores her and slides her Twiglet body into the only remaining empty chair. Nurse Kay places Helen's 2,500-calorie meal in front of her and tells us we can start.

"Glory be!" says Missy, ripping the foil off her tray and digging in.

I do the same. I'm so hungry I'm almost ready to eat the foil. It's like feeding time at the zoo at the Barfer end of the table, whereas down at the Starver end, only Tinka's got the foil off her tray. Bethany and Tracey (who I'm told is the same age as my mother but looks like an old crone) are still working on it. Helen's just sitting there, looking like she wishes she were back in the laundry cart.

"Next meal you better get your skinny ass to the table on time or I'll kick it into the next state," Missy warns Helen through a mouthful of sweet potato.

"That's enough, Melissa," warns Nurse Kay.

Helen just looks at Missy as if she's something that crawled out of the primordial slime. I think it has something to do with the fact that Missy is actually *eating*, something Helen takes tremendous pride in NOT doing.

The chicken is lukewarm and the zucchini is completely cold. The sweet potato is okay, though. I'm so hungry I'm shoveling food down my throat without really tasting it. I've almost finished emptying my tray before Queen Helen has even removed the foil from hers.

Nurse Kay is prowling around the table, encouraging the Starvers to eat and keeping an open eye for any attempts at hiding food. It's amazing what lengths the Starvers will go to so they don't have to consume all 2,500 calories. Yesterday Nurse Joe caught Bethany with a sock full of peas. Can you imagine walking around with peas squishing in your shoes? I mean, it's just so totally disgusting. She ended up having to drink an entire can of Ensure, even though she'd already eaten all the rest of the food on her tray. You could practically hear her brain working out how many times she would have to walk up and down the hallway to work off all those extra calories.

That's another Starver trick. They'll keep "forgetting" stuff in their room so they have to walk up and down the hall like fifteen times. They're not supposed to exercise until they put on a certain amount of weight, but most of them figure out a way to do it anyway. Take it from me — you should never underestimate the crafty ingenuity of someone with an eating disorder.

"Janie!" Nurse Kay says from behind me, so suddenly that I jump. "Put your napkin on the table!"

Argh . . . I forgot about the Napkin Rule. But who can blame me? I mean, seriously, I've had a lifetime of my mother nagging me to put my napkin on my lap when I eat. Yet here at Golden Slopes, it's a criminal offense. I tell you, if you're not crazy before you get here, you definitely *will* be by the time you've stayed a few days.

I want to protest, to explain that I didn't do it to hide food; I did it because it's a habit of a lifetime. But all I say is "sorry" and transfer the napkin from my lap to the table. Nurse Kay picks it up and shakes it to make sure I haven't hidden any food in it. As if. I'm *way* too hungry for that.

I notice that Helen is looking at me with a faint smile of what appears to be approval. I feel like shouting at her that I had my napkin on my lap because I was brought up with *good manners*. But I don't say anything. I just eat my dessert — chocolate pudding with a dollop of Reddi-wip on top.

Missy and Callie are already finished, and they're starting to get fidgety.

"I'm done, Nurse Kay," Callie says. "Can I be excused?"

"Me, too," Missy adds.

Nurse Kay inspects their empty trays and checks the floor underneath the table to make sure nothing ended up there.

"Okay, girls," she says. She glances up at the clock. "You're out of here at ten past one."

The Napkin Rule is mainly for the Starvers, but the Thirty-Minute Rule is aimed at us Barfers, the theory being that if they can stop us from sticking our fingers down our throats for at least thirty minutes after we eat, we'll lose the Urge to Purge.

Needless to say, it can get pretty ugly around here after mealtimes, with all these Barfers wandering around the dayroom desperate to get rid of the meal they just ate.

I finish the last of my dessert and, after passing Clean Plate Club inspection, I join my fellow Pukers in postprandial hell. It's amazing how food feels so good going down the hatch, but the minute it's down there and I feel at all full, I get completely desperate to make it come back up again. It's as if I can feel the calories circulating through my bloodstream, stopping only to glom on to my hips and butt. Despite the fact that I was hungry to the point of desperation before lunch, I'd give anything now to feel empty and light again.

I fling myself down on the sofa and grab one of the year-old copies of *People* magazine. You'd think if they were really trying to help us find ways of distracting ourselves from the overwhelming need to stick our fingers down our throats, they could fork out for some up-to-date magazines. I mean, the Hollywood couple that's "ENGAGED!" on the cover of the *People* I'm holding has been dis-engaged for six or seven months already. Still, I'm so desperate to think of something else that I read about their ecstatic, joyful love, even though like the Fates or an omniscient narrator in a Greek tragedy, I already know it's doomed. Anything's better than sitting here staring at the clock, willing the seconds to tick by faster.

When I'm finally allowed to leave the dayroom, all the Starvers have finished except for Helen, who sits in solitary splendor in front of an untouched tray of food.

CHAPTER TWO

July 20th, before dinner

I had to suffer through my first group session after lunch today. I swear, Dr. Pardy, who leads the group, is enough to give anyone an eating disorder. She's really pretty and has this perfect figure like she could be a model. And she must be intelligent, otherwise how would she have made it through medical school? Smart and pretty — if she weren't so nice, I'd hate her guts. As it is, I had a hard time listening to anything she said because I kept wishing I had a figure like hers and wondering why someone that beautiful and smart would choose to work with a bunch of screwups in a place like this. Maybe it was the only job she could get.

It was a Barfers-only group today, and because I was new to the group, Dr. Pardy made me intro-duce myself.

At school I'm really active in the drama club, and if I say so myself, I'm pretty good. I got lead

parts in major productions when I was only a sophomore and played Anne in The Diary of Anne Frank
this year. You can put me up on a stage in front of
an auditorium full of people, with someone else's
words in my mouth, and I won't bat an eyelid —
unless it's called for in the script. But put me in a
room with two other girls and a doctor and ask me
to talk about myself and I completely freak out. I
muttered, "Hi, my name's Janie" and then sat there
staring at the floor so I didn't have to look at
anyone.

"Why are you here at Golden Slopes, Janie?"
asked Dr. Pardy in her mellifluous voice. Not only is
she pretty and smart, but she'd make a great late
night DJ. Some people have all the luck.

When I told them all that my parents made me
come because they thought I had a problem, Dr.
Pardy asked me if I thought I had a problem. I told
her that I didn't think I did, at least not more than
anyone else at my school.

The girls were smiling. I thought it was because
they understood, but then Missy says, "De-Nile isn't
just a river in Egypt, is it now, Janie?"

She and Callie cracked up. Even Dr. Pardy
smiled.

"What are you talking about?" I asked, pissed
as all hell. It was like they went from being my Band
of Barfers, my Sisterhood of Sneaky Eaters, to my
Judge and freaking Jury in three minutes flat. I felt
like getting up and leaving, I was so mad. I thought
of all people this crowd would understand me,

because they're Barfers, too. I thought we shared the unbreakable Bond of Barferhood. Clearly, I was wrong. I miss my real friends — even though Kelsey, who knows me better than pretty much anyone, didn't understand about my need to get rid of excess calories by sticking my fingers down my throat. Of all my friends, only Nancy got that part of me.

Callie said that the first part of recovery is admitting you have a problem, like we're in some freakin' twelve-step program. If they think that's going to make me stand up and say, "I'm Janie Ryman . . . and I stick my fingers down my throat," they're going to be waiting a long time. I'm not the only girl at my school who pukes after she eats, and I know that for a fact. It's not a disease — it's a diet strategy. Some girls take diet pills; I stick my finger down my throat. What's the big deal?

Missy flops down next to me on the threadbare sofa.

"You writing a book or something?"

I flip my notebook shut so she can't see that I've just been writing about her.

"No."

If she thinks I'm going to be friendly after she made fun of me in group, she'd better think again.

"Well, jeez, you're sure writing enough."

I don't want to talk to her. Is it okay to ignore someone who's sitting right next to you? I give it a try, I really do, refusing to look in her direction and doodling on the cover of my notebook. Rows and rows of little boxes, because that's how I feel — boxed in.

Eventually, though, my inner Carole Ryman wins out. The need to behave in a socially correct manner must be genetic or something.

"We're supposed to, aren't we?" I say. "Keep a journal, that is."

"Ha! If we did everything we're *supposed* to, we wouldn't be locked up in this place, would we?"

I guess she has a point there.

"But doesn't Dr. Pardy ... you know ... check, or something?" I ask.

Missy cracks up.

"What, like your second-grade teacher checking that you've done your homework? No way! It's *personal*. Only if you want to 'share.'"

She does the little quote thing with her fingers when she says "share." Me, I think I'd rather die than "share."

"Well, how was I supposed to know that?" I say. "Dr. Pardy made such a big deal about how we're supposed to write down our feelings and ..."

"Yeah, yeah, she gives that speech to *all* the new kids. But it's bullshit. *My* notebook has, like, three sentences written in it — and two of them say 'This place sucks.'"

"What does the third one say?"

She stretches her arms above her head and yawns.

"I don't feel like 'sharing' that just yet."

Fine. Be that way. But don't expect me to "share" with you.

"Anyway," Missy goes on, "I've never been big on writing down my innermost secrets — too much risk."

"Risk of what?"

Missy gives me this look like I'm a few scoops of ice cream short of a sundae.

"Don't you realize that you're being observed 24/7 in this place?"

"Well, yeah, but . . ."

"The walls have ears, as they say. Everything you say and do is being noted and used to 'evaluate your current state of mind.'"

Again with the finger quotes. I'm wondering if Missy is totally paranoid or if what she says is true, in which case she's making *me* totally paranoid.

"What, even when we're not in group?"

"Anytime, anywhere," she says. "Don't say anything out loud that you wouldn't want written down in your file."

Missy gestures at my notebook.

"And be careful about what you put on paper."

I'm totally freaking out now. It's not like I want to say anything in group. I'm quite happy to sit there and let everyone else spill their guts. But not to be able to write down what I'm feeling . . . that makes me feel even more boxed in. Trapped, caged. I can't give the writing up, no matter what Missy says. I'm just going to have to make sure I keep my notebook with me at all times, even when I go to the bathroom or take a shower — that way I can be sure that no one will read it.

"Whazzup?"

Callie throws herself into the chair opposite mine and swings her legs over the arm.

"I'm just explaining to the New Girl . . ."

"Janie," I say.

"Yeah, okay, Janie, how the whole *'journaling is an important part of the therapeutic process'* bullshit is exactly that."

"So how long have you guys been here?" I ask, hoping to gain some insight into when I might escape this police state and head home to my private bathroom and my real friends.

"Five days," Missy says. "But that's five days too many, as far as I'm concerned."

"Feels like forever." Callie sighs. "But I think it's been three weeks."

I'm so horrified I can't help exclaiming, *"Three weeks?!"*

"Yeah, Callie's one of our hardcore cases," Missy says. "Out of all the eating disorder patients, I think only Helen has been here longer."

"And Tracey," Callie says. "Tinka only came a few days after me, too."

"How do you stand it?" I ask. "I've only been here *two days* and it's making me so crazy I feel like digging my way out with a spoon."

Callie laughs, but it's not a happy sound.

"Yeah, it's pretty ironic that they think being in here will make you sane, isn't it?"

"What? You don't think it's perfectly *normal* to have someone listening to you while you take a crap?" Missy says. "What's the matter with you, girl?"

"Or listening to you *trying* to take a crap," I say. "I haven't been able to since I've been in here. I think I've got stage fright."

I can't believe I'm telling two girls that I've known for all of, like, forty-eight hours about my constipation problems. Maybe I really *am* crazy.

"Oh, that happened to me, too," Missy says.

"And me," Callie adds.

I take it back. I'm not crazy. Maybe I just feel able to talk to them because we're all in this *not-able-to-take-a-shit* hole together.

"If it lasts for too much longer, you can ask Dr. Pardy to add a laxative to your medication cocktail," Missy advises me. "But I'm warning you — first she'll tell the kitchen to give you more fiber and roughage in your meals."

"Yeah, and you better warn us if that happens, so we make sure you sit near the Starvers," Callie says.

"Why is that?" I ask. "I thought seating was strictly segregated."

The two of them crack up. I'm struggling to see the joke.

"Farts," gasps Callie. "From the fiber."

"Yeah, let the Starvers suffer for a change," giggles Missy, "after making us wait so long for all our meals."

Wow. It's almost worth staying constipated just for payback. I imagine the expression on Helen's face if I let a really smelly one rip right next to her, and I start cracking up, too.

"It's a deal," I tell them.

Maybe they are my Barfing Brethren after all.

*   *   *

My parents and Harry come to visit after dinner, which is a real load of laughs.

I'm so pissed at them for sticking me in this place that part of me doesn't even want to see them. The other part wants to grab them by the knees and beg them to get me out of here tonight, so I can eat with my napkin on my lap and not have to pee with an audience outside the bathroom door. It's strange how those things make me feel so, I don't know, less than. Less than normal. Less than I should be. Less than human.

My mother hugs me and starts to cry. It's kind of embarrassing and I feel like asking her what she has to cry about, because I'm the one who's stuck in this hell-hole. I'm also afraid that her crying will be infectious, and the last thing I want to do is cry in front of the other people crowded into the dayroom for visiting hours, although I've been completely dry-eyed since I got here. I wonder if it's the meds.

"Pull yourself together, Mom," I say, extracting myself from her tentacles.

"Hey, Pussycat, how are you?" Dad says, enveloping me in his arms and hugging me to his chest.

"Don't call me that in public!" I hiss. Dad's always called me by that nickname because of my eyes, which are green and catlike. It's one thing in the privacy of our own home, where I kind of like it — although I'd never admit that to anyone — and completely another when in the presence of psycho people who aren't immediate family.

"Sorry," Dad whispers, and he lets me go. It makes me wish I hadn't said anything because I've always felt safe in one of my dad's hugs, like nothing bad could ever happen to me. But he was in on the betrayal, agreeing with Mom and Dr. Jonas, my pediatrician, that I needed "treatment." I'm still trying to work out how having someone listen outside the door while I'm trying to pee constitutes "treatment," because frankly, it just makes me feel mad and even more crazy.

"Hey, Janie," Harry says. He puts his arm around me in what approximates a hug, and his messy dark curls tickle my chin. His T-shirt smells like home, a mixture of laundry detergent and Ringo. It makes me want to keep on hugging him, but after what seems like a nanosecond he's already pulling away.

"How's Horatio?" I ask. "Are you remembering to feed him? I'm not sure I could face another hamster funeral in my current mental state."

"Don't worry, he's fine," Harry says. "I've been giving him extra treats." He gives me an awkward pat on the arm, before plunking himself on the sofa and whipping out his Nintendo DS. Once he gets going into his game, you can forget about having any kind of coherent discourse with the kid, which leaves me just my parents to converse with. Oh, joy.

"So how are things, Janie?" Dad asks. He's standing next to the sofa, unwilling or unable to sit down. I think he's afraid that if he sits down, he might catch loony cooties or something. My father hates illness of any kind and has absolutely no tolerance for mental illness, which is supposedly what I've got. Dad's the kind of guy who won't even take an aspirin when he's got a fever or a headache. I dread to think about what he's going to say about all the meds they've got me on, particularly the antidepressants. My father is the High Priest of Positive Thinking; if any bad stuff happens to you, it's because you weren't thinking positively enough. Yeah, right.

"Oh, I'm just peachy," I say. "This place is a laugh a minute. It's better than Disney World."

"That's good," Mom sniffs, dabbing tears from under her eyes with a tissue in a vain attempt to salvage her mascara. "As long as they're giving you the help you need."

I clearly didn't inherit the irony gene from my mother.

Dad rolls his eyes. He might be the High Priest of Positive Thinking, but at least he understands sarcasm.

"So what treatment have you been getting so far?" he asks.

"Well, let's see," I say. "I've had my blood pressure and temperature checked."

"We're shelling out a five hundred dollars-a-day co-pay to get you treatment and all they've done is take your temperature and check your blood pressure?"

It sounds like Dad's in strong need of getting *his* blood pressure checked. My father is very bottom-line oriented. I think it's from working so hard to make rich people richer all day.

"Don't worry — that's not all," I assure him. "They also listen outside the bathroom door, which I have to keep cracked open all of the time I'm in there, and yell at me for putting my napkin in my lap."

I'm hoping that if I can convince Dad he's not getting his money's worth, he'll tell Mom and the Golden Slopes people they have to let me go home. It looks like what I've said is having the desired effect because Dad mutters, "What kind of joint is this? I'm going to find the doctor in charge."

"Leave it, Hal, please," Mom pleads. My mother would sell her firstborn child (i.e., me) to avoid "making a scene." It's hard to imagine how she ever survived in hedge fund management.

Just then GI Joe comes into the dayroom. Dad takes one look at the muscular physique encased in Joe's nurse uniform, leans down, and hisses, "Tell me they don't have that guy listening outside your bathroom door — if they do, I'll sue the bastards."

It's kind of nice to see my dad so protective of me. It almost makes me feel like he really cares.

"Get a life, Dad!" I say. "Of course they don't let Joe listen outside the bathroom if it's a girl in there."

"Thank goodness for small mercies," Dad says, although I almost get the impression that his relief is tempered by disappointment that there's one less thing to argue with the doctors about. He straightens his tie, the equivalent of a medieval knight putting on his helmet, and is about to go raise hell about medical incompetence when my mother grabs his hand and gazes up at him with teary eyes.

"Please, Hal. Don't make a scene," she pleads again. When Mom dies, I swear that's what is going to be engraved on her tombstone. *Here lies Carole Baird Ryman. She never made a scene.*

"We have to trust the doctors know what they're doing," Mom continues. "They're the ones who specialize in treating these things."

These things. My mother, the Queen of Denial, can't even say the words out loud. I wonder what she's telling her friends about my sudden disappearance from home. I bet she's told them I'm at some exclusive drama camp. I mean, Heaven forbid that anyone might suspect that all is not perfect in the Kingdom of Ryman.

Dad gives Mom that half-angry, half-amused look. That *Honey, it's sweet and even somewhat amusing when you voice opinions, but now you should just shut up and let me get on with it* kind of look.

"Relax, sweetheart," he says, using his free hand to cup her cheek while he extracts his other hand from her clutches. "I won't make a scene. I just want to have a full and frank discussion about how exactly they are treating Janie."

He marches out of the dayroom, giving Joe the hairy eyeball as he passes by. Joe, fortunately, seems impervious to Dad's suspicious glare as he stands near the door surveying the room.

There are so many questions I want to ask my mother: Have Jenny and Clarissa taken out a contract on me? Have any of my friends called, and if so, what has she told them? Have the doctors told her when they're going to let me come home?

But Mom's sitting on the sofa opposite me, sniffling daintily into her handful of tissues.

"I'm okay, Mom," I lie. "Really. It's all fine."

I move to sit next to her on the sofa and put my arm around her shoulders. As I start rubbing her back, I suddenly wonder why I'm comforting her and not the other way around. I mean, I'm the one who is locked up here. She gets to go home and sleep in her very own king-size bed with 600-thread-count Egyptian cotton sheets, whereas I'm stuck in a narrow single bed with sheets that smell like industrial bleach. But that's the way it is with Mom. If you have a cold, she has to have the flu.

This realization causes a strange feeling in the pit of my stomach. I wonder what I would have to do, how far I'd have to go, to make Mom admit that I'm doing worse than she is. But I'm distracted from this thought when someone I've never seen before walks into the dayroom accompanied by Nurse Kay and two other adults I assume are his parents. He's a skinny guy with blond hair (Starver? Barfer? Or just Generally Psycho?) wearing a Mets shirt and sweats.

The guy he's with looks like he played football in college. He's got white hair, so he's probably older than my dad, but he's still in great shape. His arms are strong and muscley. Unlike Dad, he doesn't even have the slightest trace of a gut sticking out over his perfectly creased chinos.

The woman, without a doubt, is Blondie Boy's mother. He has her fine bone structure and slender build, not to mention her deep blue eyes and blond hair.

"This is the dayroom, Tom, where you'll eat,

have some of your group therapy sessions, and where your family visits take place," Nurse Kay tells Blondie Boy.

"So how long do you expect Tommy to be in this place?" Football Dad asks.

"It's impossible to predict," Nurse Kay replies. "It depends on the individual, and how hard he's willing to work to get well."

"Tommy'll work real hard — won't you, boy?" his dad says, thumping him on the back. "Soccer practice starts in three weeks."

I think I see Tommy-boy wince, but I can't be sure. One thing I *do* see is him giving his mother a pleading glance, but she either doesn't see it or pretends not to. I wonder if she's employing the Carole Ryman tactic: *If I make believe the problem isn't there, maybe it will go away.* It's pretty clear that if I'm my family's problem child, Tommy-boy bears that honor in his. It makes me feel an instant kinship.

"I hope your father isn't getting into a fight with the doctor," Mom says, twisting the wad of mascara-smudged tissues between her manicured fingers.

Yes! I think. A reason to escape Mom's tearful clutches.

"I'll go check," I tell her, leaping off the sofa before she can protest or Harry can volunteer to go instead. As if. He's glued to his Nintendo — I swear, those things are like crack for boys his age.

I head out into the hallway and immediately hear Dad's raised voice down by the nurses' station. I've heard enough arguments at home over the last twelve months to last me a lifetime, so I head in the opposite direction toward the TV room, which consists of one large TV that everyone has to fight over and several couches that have seen better days.

Unfortunately, the Generally Psycho folks have control of the remote tonight, and they've opted to watch *Saving Private Ryan*. Talk about a bizarre choice of movie for a bunch of depressed people. Even though I know it's supposed to be a great movie about war and stuff, I can't stand watching blood, gore, and guts. But I don't want to deal with Dad's fighting or Mom's tears, so I just sit on the floor outside the TV room with my head on my knees, listening to the sounds of people getting shot and maimed.

"Um . . . are you okay?"

I look up and there's Blondie Boy staring down at me, looking worried.

"Yeah, I'm okay," I say. "I just don't want to hang out with my visiting parents. But on the other hand, I don't particularly want to see people's intestines hanging out, either."

Blondie pokes his head into the TV room, sees what's on the screen, and emerges laughing.

"I see what you mean. Seems like a strange choice of movie for a place like this, don't ya think?"

"Exactly what I was just thinking," I say. "I'm Janie, by the way."

"Tom," he says.

"So I gathered. I was in the dayroom when you came in with Nurse Kay."

A slow red flush spreads up his neck and over his face.

"Great. So my parents have preceded me in your impression."

"Listen, dude, that's my dad you can hear down the hall telling the doctors they don't know their ass from their elbow. So don't think you're the only one with pro-genitor problems."

He laughs, showing even white teeth. Cool. He has a good command of vocabulary. I like that in a guy.

"So what are you in for?" Tom says. It sounds like a prison movie question. *I got ten years for donut consump-tion and fraud.*

"Persistent Puking," I tell him. "You?"

He hesitates for a minute, then says, "I passed out when I was doing sprints with Dad. I said it was just heat exhaustion, but Mom took me to the doctor and he said . . . well . . ."

Instead of finishing his sentence, he just lifts up the Mets shirt and, I swear, you can see the outline of every single rib. Damn. I was hoping he was one of us.

"A Starver," I say.

"That's what the doctor told my mother. Dad doesn't believe it. He says anorexia is a girl disease."

"It's fair to say that you are the only guy Starver in here," I tell him. "But there are plenty of Generally Psycho guys, so don't worry about not having anyone to hang out with."

"That's okay," Tom says. "I'm not really in the mood for being with people right about now." He blushes again. "Present company excluded, of course."

"Well, Tom, I'll be your best friend and play with you every day as long as you promise me one simple thing," I tell him.

"Okay, what?"

"Whatever you do...make SURE you're on time for lunch."

CHAPTER THREE

July 21st

I've been wondering: Why do some people end up being Barfers and others Starvers? Or all the other weird ways of eating in between, like people who binge eat but don't puke, or eat and then exercise for three hours, or pop diet pills to help them not eat? When you think about it, there's a wealth of ways you can be screwed up about food and eating — or not eating, as the case might be. What makes someone turn into a Helen, a Bethany, or a Tom instead of a Missy or a Callie — or a me, for that matter? Is it a different gene for Barfing and another one for Starving?

I can't imagine being a Starver. I like food too much. Well, that's not exactly true. I guess I have what you might call a love-hate relationship with food — love to eat it but hate to have eaten it. As soon as I finish eating, it's like this tape starts playing in my head: "You are SO FAT! What the hell did you eat that for? You're such a pig. No one is ever going to like you because you're just so disgusting and they'll get ill just looking at you." Then all I can think about is how quickly I can get to a bathroom to puke, because puking is the only thing that seems to make the tape stop . . . at least till the next time I'm full.

Was there ever a period of time when I was able to love food unreservedly, without thinking of it as "the enemy" the minute it was in my stomach? When I was a little girl, was I like Harry, constantly running to Mom to beg for cookies? Was there a time when I could go to birthday parties and eat a slice of cake without feeling guilty, like I was doing something bad? Was I able to eat a bar of chocolate without hearing that critical voice in my head?

If there was such a time, it's been lost in a haze of constant dieting and bingeing, overtaken by all the hours I've spent gazing down the toilet bowl while sticking my fingers down my throat.

What is it like being at your family's dinner table? Discuss.

That's the question Dr. Pardy has posed to the group this morning. It's a joint Starver–Barfer assemblage. Helen and her skinny minions are clustered on sofas by the window. Callie, Missy, and I are on the opposite side of the room, in Pukerville. One thing I learned pretty quickly is that there's a sort of seating apartheid in this place. After only three days, I've learned that we Barfers need to stick together.

When Tom walks in, you can almost feel the frisson of shock, as if some naked guy has walked into the girls' locker room. Tinka starts whispering in Bethany's ear. Missy lets out a wolf whistle. You'd think they'd never seen a guy before.

Tom's face turns ripe tomato; he looks like he would rather be anywhere but here, and I sure know *that* feeling. So I catch his eye and gesture to the empty armchair next to me.

"You *know* him already?" Callie says, nudging my ribs with her elbow. "You're a fast worker."

For some reason this makes me really pissed. I mean, all I did was offer the guy a chair; it's not like I jumped his bones or anything. Tom's SO not my type. He's too thin, for one thing. I could never go out with someone who's thinner than I am, because I'd be obsessing the entire time over whether he thought I was fat — even more than I normally obsess about being fat, which is a lot. Besides, Tom's just too — I don't know — *pretty*, with his blond hair and high cheekbones. He and Missy would be a great pair — I can just see them living in a four-bedroom colonial in Darien complete with perfectly trimmed lawn, white picket fence, and a minivan full of blond-haired, blue-eyed brats.

I tell Callie to shut up and then introduce Tom to the Barfers sitting on the sofa with me. Callie's revving up to interrogate him when Dr. Pardy comes in and announces that we're going to talk about what it's like to eat meals at home.

Now there's something I'd rather not think about. It's bad enough to have to *eat* dinner at my house without having to *talk* about it, too.

31

So what's it like? Well, let's see — it depends on if Dad gets home from work on time or if he's late. Scenario A: Dad makes it home from work. As soon as we're all sitting around the table comes the inevitable: "So, how was school today?" Predictable question, to which I give an equally predictable answer: "Fine." Once in a while Dad gets mad at me for the monosyllabic response, but most of the time I think he just chalks it up to teenagerhood. Harry is too young to have caught on to my strategy, so he launches into a lengthy diatribe about the injustice of homework and how much he hates his math teacher. Once Dad has half-listened to Harry, he launches into telling Mom about his day, and Harry and I are basically out of his consciousness unless we start fighting or use bad table manners.

Scenario B: Dad says he's going to make it home from work on time, but doesn't. Mom stomps around the kitchen, sighing and huffing every time she looks at the clock. Harry whines that he's hungry. We wait around until we're all famished enough to eat Purina Dog Chow and finally Mom says we might as well go ahead and eat before all her slaving away over a hot stove goes to waste. I'm so hungry I stuff my face until my stomach seems to expand about six inches over the top of my jeans. Then I can't wait to get away from the table to puke so it doesn't stay that way.

Scenario C: Dad's away on a business trip, so we just have a simple dinner on time. This is my second favorite scenario.

Scenario D: Mom's going out, so she says Harry and I can just order pizza. This is my completely favorite scenario, because the two of us eat in the den while we watch TV, and that's way better than being stuck at the dinner table being forced to listen to the latest fluctuations in the stock market. But pizza's one of those foods that I always scarf too much of; inevitably, I puke it up during a commercial. Sometimes, when I'm really bad, I eat another piece after I've puked up the first few. Then I puke that one up, too.

So there it is: what it's like to eat at Casa del Ryman. *Get it in, get it over with, and get it out* — that's my motto.

"Before we start, we've got a new group member," says Dr. Pardy. "Tom, why don't you tell us a little bit about yourself and why you're here?"

Poor Tom looks like he wishes he could melt into the armchair.

"Uh . . . my name's Tom," he says, kind of unnecessarily since Dr. Pardy just told everyone his name. I can see his hand shaking where it rests on his jean-clad knee. I feel like taking hold of it for moral support, but I couldn't bear the flak I'd get from Callie. Plus we're not supposed to get all touchy-feely with the other patients. It's another one of the many Golden Rules here at Golden Slopes.

"I — I — I'm here because, well, I guess . . . because they tell me I'm anorexic."

He gets strange looks from some of the Starvers because he's sitting in Pukerville.

I can feel the denial question coming on. After only a few days in this place, I've already got the hang of being crazy.

"And do *you* think you're anorexic, Tom?" Dr. Pardy asks.

Tom looks down at the floor, like there's something completely fascinating there.

"I dunno. Maybe . . . well, I guess."

Okay, Tommy-boy's had his "I'm Tom and I'm a Starver" moment. Can we move on, please?

"So, Tom, what are some of the things you enjoy doing, when you're not at Golden Slopes?" asks Dr. Pardy.

"Well, I play soccer, but I'm not sure I'd say I *enjoy* it."

"So why do you do it then?" asks Missy. I still can't get used to the fact that this angel-faced girl can be so blunt.

"I — I . . . well, I guess because my dad expects me to," Tom says.

"And you *always* do what your parents tell you to do?" Callie asks, dripping scorn. This doesn't surprise me. From the conversations I've had with Callie so far, I get the impression she's the kind of girl who'd do the exact *opposite* of what her parents tell her to do.

I want to tell her to leave Tom alone. I don't know why I feel so protective of him. Maybe I just feel like every-one's giving him an unnecessarily hard time on his first day — sort of like they did to me. I mean, who died and made them shrinks?

"No," Tom says, looking even more miserable. "I don't. But soccer is different."

"How is soccer different?" Dr. Pardy asks.

"Because it's something I do with my dad," Tom says. "Because ever since I can remember, sports are the only thing my dad talks to me about. Playing soccer, watching football and baseball, and going to games are what we do together."

"But what do *you* enjoy doing, Tom?" Dr. Pardy asks, not giving up.

"I don't know," Tom mumbles. "I guess . . ."

It's almost as if you can see this internal struggle going on inside Tom's head — like there's a little angel on one side saying, "Do it! Be honest!" and there's a little devil on the other side saying, "No! Don't tell them! They'll laugh!" His knee starts tapping up and down furiously.

"I . . . like going into the city. To art museums and concerts and stuff like that. I do that kind of thing with my mom and sometimes my sister. Oh, and I like to read. I read a lot."

"What kind of books do you like?" I ask him.

"Pretty much anything," he says. "Fiction, nonfiction, magazines, newspapers. Comics. Cereal boxes. If it's got words, I'll read it."

"Well, I'd like to encourage you to put your own words on paper, Tom," says Dr. Pardy. "Journaling is a very important piece of the therapeutic process here at Golden Slopes."

I wonder if she really believes that journaling will help or if she's just encouraging us to write because someday she's going to use our journals to write a book — *My Life Among the Crazy People*. Maybe I should start writing in code. Or maybe I'm just being paranoid. But you know what they say: *Just because you're paranoid, doesn't mean they aren't out to get you.*

After the "journaling is therapy" speech, it's on to our family mealtimes. It's weird; all of us have some issue with meals. I guess that should come as no surprise seeing as we're all in this joint for eating problems. Missy says she hates being at the same table as her stepfather, because he's a creep who's always picking on her and her younger brother, Chris, so she just eats as fast as she can so she can get away. Bethany's mom always says stuff like, "Are you sure you want seconds of mashed potatoes? They've got 36.8 grams of carbs per serving!" Apparently she keeps a laptop in the kitchen so she can look up the calorie and carb content of everything she or any of her kids put in their mouths. No wonder the girl is a complete basket case about food.

Dr. Pardy lets whoever wants to talk go first. She somehow manages to maintain some kind of eye contact with whomever is speaking, while writing stuff down on the yellow pad on her clipboard. That yellow pad is part of the reason I don't like to speak up. I'm afraid she's going to write down that I'm a complete screwup and I'll end up stuck in this place for the rest of my natural life.

The problem is, once all the voluntary "sharing" is over with, Dr. Pardy moves on to those of us for whom talking to the group about our personal secrets is a form of purgatory. Take Tracey, for example. She's the oldest person in the room, including Dr. Pardy, and she looks like the oldest person in the universe. Her skin is all dried out and leathery, and her arms are covered in hair, while the hair on her head is thin, stringy, and dull. Like Helen, she always wears sweats and long sleeves, even though it's like ninety degrees and humid out, and the air-conditioning doesn't work so well so it's pretty warm inside, too. She keeps to herself most of the time — I've only ever seen her at group or at mealtimes.

"Tracey, how are mealtimes for you when you're at home?" Dr. Pardy asks.

Tracey seems to retreat into her sweatshirt like a turtle into its shell. I haven't paid a whole lot of attention to her before because she's so much older than the rest of us, but I suddenly wonder what would make a grown-up stop eating. In my experience, it's usually the grown-ups who are telling us younger folks what and when to eat.

"Empty," Tracey says. It's hard to hear her because she speaks in a voice scarcely louder than a whisper.

"What do you mean by 'empty'?" Dr. Pardy asks.

"I don't know," Tracey whispers, looking more turtle-like by the minute.

"Sure you do," Callie says. "Otherwise you wouldn't have said it. So spit it out."

One thing you can say about Callie, she doesn't beat about the bush. She just comes out and says stuff the rest of us might think but wouldn't dare say. There are times I hate that about her, like in that first group session. But then I think about what it would feel like to have guts like her, and wonder if I hang around her long enough whether some of it will rub off on me.

"Well, after my husband left me . . ." Tracey says. She stops and suddenly there are tears moistening her dry cheeks.

It's so weird to see her being emotional. She's just been this quiet, older peripheral being, almost a nonpresence. I'm struck by the sudden realization that underneath the baggy sweats and the old crone exterior Tracey's a hurting person, just like the rest of us.

"I didn't have any appetite after he left. He left me for his younger . . . and . . . *thinner* coworker. I kept thinking that if I'd been smarter, if I'd been prettier, if I'd only been younger and thinner, if I'd been a better wife, a better — well, a better *everything*, then he wouldn't have fallen for her and walked out on me."

Dr. Pardy stands up and walks over to Tracey with a box of tissues. They must have to buy tissues by the truckload in this place. Not that I've needed them. I'm like the Sahara of the psycho scene.

"My whole life until now I've been something to someone," Tracey sobs. "I met Paul in college and we got married as soon as we graduated. I got pregnant with Mitchell right away, and then had James eighteen months later. I've never worked other than summer jobs and babysitting. Now the boys are grown up and don't need me, and my ex-husband doesn't need me either. I'm . . . I'm just . . . *worthless*."

I feel so sorry and sad for Tracey. How awful her life must be! It makes me never want to get married, just in case my husband ditches me. Like my dad ditched Clarissa. I don't ever want to feel the kind of pain Tracey feels.

"You're not worthless, Tracey," Bethany says, patting Tracey's skinny, sweatpant-covered knee. "You've got so much to offer."

"Like what?!" Tracey shouts. "I've got absolutely nothing to offer! If I died tomorrow, everyone would just be better off!"

I jump, because her rage is so sudden, and loud, her self-loathing so vehement and strong I can almost feel it storm over me. Is this invisible Tracey, who never speaks above a whisper?

But then she shrinks back into her normal, turtle self.

"If I'm not Paul's wife and Mitchell and James's mother, then what am I?" she asks in a tremulous whisper. "I'm nothing. That's what I am — nothing."

The room is quiet except for the sound of Tracey weeping. Even Missy, who always seems to have something to say, is silent. What can anyone say in the presence of that much grief?

"Tracey, if you could choose to be something, what would it be?" asks Dr. Pardy.

"I don't *know*. I've never been anything but a wife and a mother."

"What about when you were a little girl?" Dr. Pardy says. "Was there something you wanted to be when you were growing up?"

Tracey laughs bitterly through her tears. "I wanted to get married and have kids."

Callie snorts, like she can't imagine anyone wanting so little out of life. Dr. Pardy gives her a quieting look.

I guess it must have been different when Tracey was a girl. It's not like I *don't* want to get married and have kids — well, okay, the idea of getting married is kind of scary, I'll admit, but I still want to do it someday. It's just there's so much else I want to do besides. Like I want to backpack around Europe instead of staying in luxury hotels with my parents and I want to drive across the United States from Key West to Seattle in a convertible and I want to go to college and star in a movie and have a boyfriend who really likes me, likes me for *me*, unlike Matt Lewis. And I want never to be stuck in a place like this ever again.

"What about hobbies? Have you ever had any hobbies?" Dr. Pardy persists. I have to give her credit — I don't know how she remains so patient when faced with someone who is so clueless about herself.

Tracey twists a tissue until it looks like a small, about-to-disintegrate sausage in her trembling fingers.

"I don't know . . . I . . ." she sniffs. "I guess I used to like to make clothes. I used to make all my own clothes when I was growing up and in college — up till after James was born. I didn't have time to sew after that, and by the time I did, Paul was doing so well at work that I just bought everything we needed instead of making it."

"How did it make you feel to make your own clothes?" Dr. Pardy asks.

"Good — like I'd accomplished something," Tracey says.

"It might seem like we've gotten off track here, but we haven't," Dr. Pardy says. "Eating disorders often result from a feeling of worthlessness or, as Tracey describes it, 'emptiness,' and in order to combat that feeling, it's important to work out who we are and what we want out of life."

She looks around the room from over her geek-chic glasses, which just make her look like Teacher Barbie. Today she's wearing beige linen capris and a tailored safari jacket and she looks like she just stepped out of the pages of *Vogue*.

"We've got to wrap this up now, but for homework I want all of you to make a list of ten words you would use to describe yourself and ten words you think your friends or family would use to describe you. We'll discuss them tomorrow."

She turns to Tracey, who is back in silent-turtle mode. "Thank you for sharing with us, Tracey. It was very brave."

As everyone else gets up to leave, I ask Tom, "So what did you think?" He's sitting glued to the chair, looking shell-shocked by it all.

"I feel so sorry for her," he murmurs back. "Her husband must be a world-class bastard."

I'm taken aback by his vehemence. I'd have thought he'd have a guy perspective on it — you know, like *Good for him trading in boring old Tracey for a younger, prettier model*. But it's not like that. His fists are clenched like he wants to punch someone.

"Janie, are you coming? It's *Let the Animals Out to Smoke* time," Callie says.

We're only allowed outside for two half-hour breaks morning and afternoon, which drives smokers like Callie nuts. I miss the fresh air, although I don't get to have much of it when I'm out in the courtyard hanging with the smokers. But since Callie and Missy are the closest I have to friends in this place, it's worth inhaling a little bit of passive smoke.

"I'll be out in a minute," I tell her. She gives me a really obvious wink, and she and Missy leave, whispering and giggling about me and my nonexistent romance with Tom.

"My dad always says it takes two people to make a marriage and two people to break it," I tell him, when we're alone. "He should know — his first one broke up."

"Sometimes it's more one person's fault than the other," Tom says, his face stony.

I'm totally getting the impression that there's more to this story than meets the eye.

"Like, how?"

I can almost hear his brain working, wondering if he trusts me enough to tell me whatever it is that's making him so mad. I find myself really hoping that he does. I might not be attracted to Tom, but I feel a connection to him somehow. Maybe it's because we both have loud, obnoxious dads.

"My dad cheats," Tom mutters, staring at a spot on the puke-green linoleum floor as if it were the ceiling of the Sistine Chapel. "I saw him once with one of his girlfriends."

I take a deep breath in, trying to think of something I can say, but my mind's a total blank.

"I was out with my friends — we were supposed to see a movie but the one we wanted to see was sold out, so we took the bus downtown to go hang at the Javanet Café."

Tom's skinny knee starts moving up and down again, a mile a minute. I want to put my hand on it so it'll stop, but I get the impression he needs to move it in order to talk.

"We were passing by this little Italian restaurant, and I was checking my reflection in the window to see how I looked because Jo — well, a friend of mine — was supposed to be hanging down at the Javanet, and I saw my dad holding hands with this blond chick and looking all lovey-dovey."

I tried to imagine what I would do under those circumstances. Would I confront Dad? Would I tell Mom?

"Did you tell your dad you saw him?" I asked.

Tom laughs, but it's a sour sound, not a funny one.

"No. I was too much of a coward to confront him. And now every time I look at my mom, I think, 'You poor sucker. He's going to dump you.' Because the weird thing is, this chick looks like a dead ringer for Mom from her wedding photos."

"That *is* weird," I agree. "You'd think he'd at least go for something different if he's going to mess around on your mom. You know, variety is the spice of life and all that."

"But the worst thing is that, try as I might, I can't ever remember seeing my dad look at my mom the way he was looking at this younger mom clone. Okay, maybe in pictures from when they were first married, but never in real life. So I'm wondering if my parents were ever really happy together . . . or if their whole marriage has just been one big lie."

I wish I knew what to say to Tom, but I don't. This is too big for me. And if it's too big for me, a total stranger, it must be an unbearable burden for Tom to be toting around — this secret about his dad that he knows will devastate his mom, and having to look at them both every day.

"C'mon, let's go out and inhale some fresh air laced with passive smoke," I say, because it's the only thing I can think of to take his mind off it.

"Thanks, but I think I'm just going to lie down for a while."

I want to argue with him, to tell him that he should be around people instead of being miserable by himself — but I don't. I want to hug him — but I don't. I want to tell him that I can't imagine how he's able to get up in the morning carrying a monkey that size on his back — but I don't. I don't do anything except say, "Okay, see you later." Then I go outside and think about all the things I could have done or said to try to make him feel better, but didn't. And I hate myself even more.

CHAPTER FOUR

July 21st, evening

It's time to do my homework for Dr. Pardy. It's easy to come up with ten words that describe how I see me:

Fat.

Sad.

Bulimic.

Screwed up.

Defective.

Smart.

Ugly.

Empty.

Confused.

Scared.

It's a lot harder to come up with ten words that describe how my friends and my family see me. I guess I'll come up with five adjectives for each. First for the bad news — in other words, my family. From Mom and Dad I'd say: difficult, moody, and dramatic. Perfect Jenny and Clarissa would contribute spoiled and selfish to the list.

My friends, on the other hand, would probably be more positive about what I have to offer the world. Take Kelsey, for instance. She's my best friend, or at least she was. I have to let myself think she still is, because the alternative is too awful to think about. It'll be hard enough to face going back to school in September — that's if they let me out of here by then — but the thought of doing it without Kelsey's friendship — argh. Well, I'll try to channel some good Hal Ryman positivity here and assume she is still my best friend, in which case I think her words would be funny and loyal. Nancy, my drama friend, on the other hand, would say I'm shy and insecure. I think that's because she's seen a side of me that no one else has, not even Kelsey. And Danny . . . well, Danny would probably say I'm smart and pretty, but he's not exactly objective because we've been friends since our first day of nursery school. Seriously, the guy asked me to marry him, back when we were three. I bet he wouldn't do it now, though, after what happened. For some reason that fills me with sadness so heavy I feel smothered by the weight of it.

Now that I look at these words, it strikes me how differently I think my friends see me than how I think my family sees me. I guess that's why they say "You can't pick your family but you can pick your friends." If my parents could make a choice between me and a different daughter, would they *still pick me? Somehow I doubt it. It's not like they've never said they love me, or anything like that. They have. I'm just not sure that I'd pick me, if I had the choice.*

Another thing I notice from looking at these words is how differently I see myself from the way everyone else sees me. I'm afraid of how my friends see me, even though they seem to view me better than I do myself, because I'm scared to death that one day they'll wake up and realize that I'm none of those things, that I'm not as nice a person as they think I am, that they've been wrong about me all along. Then they'll dump me.

On the other hand, I'm scared to death that I really AM all the bad things that my parents and Perfect Jenny think I am. Then I couldn't blame anyone for dumping me — even my own parents.

I've been thinking a lot about Tom since this afternoon. I wonder how he manages to get out of bed every morning knowing he has to carry the weight of his father's affair around — especially since his mom doesn't know. I mean, if she knew and his parents were fighting about it all the time and throwing things, then maybe it wouldn't be so bad. At least everyone would know where they stood, instead of having to go around playing Happy Families when they know it's all a lie. It must be so hard for Tom to have to keep that secret growing inside of him like an undiagnosed tumor. The fact that he was willing to share that secret with me when he hasn't told anyone else, when he barely even knows me, makes me feel incredibly special, like he's given me a gift of trust. I feel kind of bad, though — because I'm not sure I'll be able to give it back.

I've also been thinking about Mom and Dad and Clarissa and Perfect Jenny. Mom used to work with Dad — she was a vice president at Bayview Partners and about a year ago Perfect Jenny told me that they were having an affair and that's the reason Dad and Clarissa got divorced. It freaked me out at the time, because I never realized that Mom was the "Other Woman." I always thought that Dad and Clarissa were already divorced when my parents started dating. I felt ashamed, like it was somehow my fault, and I hated Jenny for making me feel that way. It also made me wonder if that's why Perfect Jenny has always lorded her grades and her competence in everything over me. I resolved to try not to get mad at her when she's her usual condescending self. That lasted all of about . . . I don't know, three minutes.

After that conversation with Tom, I can't stop thinking about how it must have felt for Jenny when her parents were getting divorced. Like did she ever go to the mall with her friends and run into Dad buying sexy underwear with Mom in Victoria's Secret? (A completely revolting thought, I know, but if she was his "Other Woman," then it's not out of the question, is it?) Or did Jenny just come home from school one day and have Clarissa

tell her that Dad was leaving — BANG! SURPRISE! —
that he was divorcing them to move in with Mom?

You would think Perfect Jenny would hate
Mom because of that, but they get along better
with each other than either of them does with me.
It's bad enough that Dad prefers Jenny, but at least
she's his own flesh and blood. Mom's got no
excuse — unless it's that I'm so awful that even the
daughter of someone she loathes as much as she
does Clarissa is preferable. Not a pleasant thought.

I wonder if the reason why Dad was so deter-
mined to go all out and give Perfect Jenny the
Perfect Wedding was to make it up to her for hav-
ing that affair with Mom and leaving Clarissa. Ha!
Well, thanks to me, the Perfect Wedding wasn't
quite so perfect, was it?

I wonder if they'll ever forgive me.

We're not allowed to have cell phones, computers, or
iPods in this joint, which seriously sucks. Haven't these
guys heard of "Friends and Family"? Do they think we're
living in the Stone Age?

Anyway, to talk to anyone we have to line up in the
hallway to use the very public pay phone. Forget about
talking privately to your boyfriend — if you're lucky
enough to have one, which I'm not. I mean, at one point
I believed that I did, but I found out — pretty brutally, I
might add — at Perfect Jenny's wedding that the guy
I *thought* was my boyfriend didn't seem to share the opin-
ion. Not in the slightest.

I've decided that since I've been in here a few days already I need to call Kelsey. This is the longest time I haven't spoken, e-mailed, or IM'd her in forever. I think I'm going through withdrawal, especially since the last time we spoke . . . well, let's just say we didn't exactly part on the best of terms. So I grab the roll of quarters my parents left me when they visited and head for the pay phone. There's always a line, but at least this morning it's not too bad; I end up being third in line after Helen, who is wearing what looks like four sweatshirts and *still* manages to look like a stick insect. Her eyes are sunken and hollow looking and it's like she's on a different planet, staring ahead dazed and unfocused. Knowing her, she's probably counting up the calories she had to eat yesterday and is thinking about how she can avoid consuming any today. Her thin legs move up and down in her baggy sweats, which after three days in this place I now know to be an attempt to burn off calories — like she really needs to burn off any more.

"Hey, Helen," I say. "What's up?"

Psych ward etiquette requires that you never ask "How are you?" because it's such a stupid question. I mean, if we were okay, we wouldn't be in here, would we?

I can't tell if she doesn't hear me or if she's just being rude and ignoring me, because at first she doesn't answer — in fact, she doesn't even look in my direction, just keeps her skinny legs pumping. But then I hear her whisper *498, 499, 500,* and I realize she's been counting, because after she hits *500,* her legs stop moving and she turns to face me.

"Nothing. What's ever up in this fucking hellhole?"

50

I'm a little taken aback. It's the first time I've heard Helen curse. It's the first time I've even heard Helen sound angry. Usually, it's like she's got the same supernatural control over her emotions that she has over her calorie intake. I'm still trying to think of a reply when the person who's on the phone hangs up and says "all yours" to Helen.

Helen digs a bunch of quarters out of the pocket of her sweats (I bet her weight just halved) and feeds them into the phone.

I'm trying not to listen, but when someone is on the phone right next to you, it's kind of hard not to.

"Hi, Dad, it's me. . . . So when are you going to get me out of here?" she says.

I can't hear her dad's response, but I assume it's something she doesn't want to hear, because she looks even less happy than she did before she made the call.

"But it's not like they're actually *doing* anything for me in here and . . . Dad, I can't take being here anymore. I've been stuck in this dump for six weeks already and it sucks. *Please* get me out. I'm *begging* you . . ."

Six weeks? Please tell me I won't be in here for *that* long. I'll die.

Helen sounds like she's about to cry.

"Well, if you're not going to get me out of here, are you at least going to come visit? . . . But you haven't been here in *weeks* — neither has Mom. . . . Aren't I more important to you than some stupid business trip?"

She takes a deep breath. "Yeah, right. . . . You just don't love me." Then she's screaming down the phone, "You've *never* loved me! You —"

All of a sudden she drops to the floor. Her eyes roll back in her head and her twiglike arms and legs twitch like a bug that's been sprayed with Raid. Her father's voice is still buzzing from the handset. Everything seems like it's in slow motion before my mind registers what's happening and I open my mouth and start to scream for help, for the nurses, for *anyone*.

Joe is the first nurse to hit the scene.

"CODE RED! *Get the crash cart!*" he shouts, falling to his knees beside Helen and feeling for a pulse in her neck.

He starts pumping on Helen's chest with his beefy arms, so hard I'm worried he's going to break her.

All hell is breaking loose. Nurses come running from every which way. Nurse Kay sees me standing there.

"Janie, go to your room and shut the door!"

"But please, I need to make sure Helen's okay and . . ."

"NOW, Janie!" Nurse Kay shouts. "Get to your room, NOW!"

And I thought Nurse Kay was one of the good guys. I run down the hall to my room and slam the door behind me. Then I curl up on my bed, clutching my decrepit old teddy bear, Mr. Cuddles, scared shitless and wondering if Helen is going to be okay. I mean, she can be a complete bitch and she pisses me off when she hides and we have to wait to eat meals, but I don't want her to *die* or anything.

It feels like I'm stuck in my room forever. I can hear stuff going on down the hall, but not well enough to know what's happening with Helen. When I first got here, I was glad that I didn't have a roommate, in case she was a bitch or snored or something. But I sure as hell wish I had one now, because at least then I'd have someone to talk to about what's going on.

Instead all I can think about is the fridge at home, and what I would be eating from it right now if I weren't confined to my room inside this prison. I'd start with the freezer, the Ben & Jerry's Chocolate Therapy ice cream. I'd check to see if there was any chocolate syrup in the fridge, and if so, I'd pour it straight into the tub of Ben & Jerry's and maybe even cover it with Reddi-wip. Then I'd see if there were any brownies or chocolate-chip cookies, or maybe some of that Belgian chocolate that Mom buys from Whole Foods.

My imagination of what I would eat is so vivid that after I've worked my way through my mind's freezer and refrigerator, I feel like I have to purge, even though I haven't really eaten anything. My stomach feels bloated and distended, like it does after I binge, and the critical voice in my head starts berating me: *You fat pig! You're disgusting. I can see the rolls of fat hanging over your waistband and poking through the thighs of your jeans. You make me sick. You've just consumed like 10,000 calories in just twenty minutes and they're making a beeline for your big fat butt. I'm surprised you can even sit on that bed without breaking it you're so grossly obese. . . .* On and on and on it goes, until I feel like I have to purge or I'll die. I look around the room to see what I can throw up into without the nurses finding out. *Think! You fat slob! Think!*

Then bingo! I remember Bethany and the peas in her sock. In the top drawer of the scratched, Formica-topped dresser are several pairs of potential barf-receptacles. But how do I cover up the smell? There's something about the smell of puke that makes me want to barf. I figure I can do it near the window, which is cracked open at the top, letting in the growling hum of a lawn mower. The bottom half of the window doesn't open, to prevent us from jumping ship — or just plain jumping, because we crazy folks might just do stuff like that, you know.

Sock in hand, I pull the desk chair over to the window, climb aboard, and stick my fingers down my throat. At first I only gag, but then I feel the full-fledged barf reflex starting. I cover my mouth with the sock, which smells, strangely, of home, and regurgitate what little is in my stomach. The problem with puking when it's been a while since your last meal is that all this stomach acid comes up, too, and it really hurts your throat. Puking right after eating's a cinch. That's why they keep us Barfers away from the bathroom for so long after each meal.

The sock is filled from toe to heel with warm vomit, and I need to get rid of it before the whole room begins to stink. Since I don't plan to use *that* sock again, I decide to toss it out the window, throwing it as far out as possible, so if it's found, no one will be able to pin it on me. I hide the leftover sock inside another pair, just in case I need it at a later date. I'll have to tell Mom I need her to bring me more socks from home the next time she visits.

I feel so much better after purging. I guess that's why it's called purging — because you get the stuff that's bad out of you, and then you feel calmer and more . . . I don't know . . . pure. Empty. Like before I purged there was all this . . . stuff . . . swirling around inside me . . . so much that it felt like my brain was a socket with too many plugs, about to short-circuit. But once all the bad stuff comes out of my throat, the swirling stops and I don't feel overloaded anymore.

I know I'm supposed to be in here so they can "cure" me of doing this, but I'm not so sure I want to be cured. I don't know how to achieve that feeling of empty okayness without sticking my fingers down my throat. Sure, I don't like the actual act of throwing up. I hate it. But it's like the opposite of eating. I love eating, but hate having eaten. I hate barfing, but love having purged.

When they finally let us out of our rooms, we all have to go into the dayroom. There, a strangely pale Nurse Kay tells us that Helen had a seizure and went into cardiac arrest. She's been transferred to a hospital — a *real* hospital with an emergency room and intensive care, not just a prison-loony bin like Golden Slopes.

"Is she going to be okay?" I ask. Like I said, even though Helen can be pretty annoying, I don't want anything really *dire* to happen to her.

"That depends on Helen," says Nurse Kay grimly. "Just as all of you getting better depends on you."

I guess I'm not getting better then... because I wouldn't depend on me for anything. Not a chance.

CHAPTER FIVE

July 23rd

*I was too freaked out to write last night. I was too
freaked out to do much of anything all day
yesterday. I couldn't even bring myself to call Kelsey
because it would mean going back to the pay
phone — and, believe me, I really needed to talk to
someone other than a nurse.*

*Nurse Kay keeps trying to get me to talk
about stuff but I don't want to tell her how messed
up I feel, because I'm afraid it'll mean I have to
stay in here longer. Yesterday during the post-
dinner Thirty-Minute Rule, Callie told me how she
made some comment to Missy about cutting herself and Joe overheard it. The next thing Callie
knows, Dr. Pardy hauls her in to speak in private
and quotes what she said completely verbatim.
Callie said at first she thought Missy had narced her
out but after they had a huge fight and Missy swore
up, down, and sideways that she hadn't said a word*

to anyone, because why the hell would she, Callie realized it must have been Joe. So me — I'm keeping my mouth shut, locked as tight as the door that keeps me in this place, the door that you have to be buzzed out of to be able to reenter Normal Land.

But I keep seeing images of Helen on the floor by the pay phone with her pale face and twitching limbs. It's like I've got some silent horror movie constantly running in my brain even when I'm trying to think about other things. I keep wondering if she's all right. It's no use asking anyone around here about how she's doing, because, believe me, I've tried. Joe said he doesn't know anything; same with Nurse Kay and Nurse Rose. But I find that hard to believe. Maybe I should ask Dr. Pardy . . . except then she'll try to get me to talk about what happened. When I had to meet with her one-on-one the first day I was here, I felt like she was trying to pull the words out of my throat against my will.

Everything she asked had some hidden motivation, and anything I said would just be used as evidence that I'm crazy and need to be locked up in here indefinitely. That's part of the reason I don't want to speak up in group, or "share" the contents of this journal. What's in my head is private, and I don't want people poking there and judging me for the things I think and feel. I get enough of that at home and at school. I need to keep some of myself for myself — unsullied, uncorrupted, secret, and unsaid. Otherwise, there won't be anything left of me.

But sometimes I wonder if that's already true; there are times when I get so tired of trying to be everything to everyone I feel like shouting, "Will the real Janie Ryman please stand up?" I've spent so long striving to be as perfect as Perfect Jenny to please my parents, striving to be smart to please my teachers, but not too smart to please boys, striving to fit in, striving to be thin, striving to be pretty. I'm not sure I even know what the real Janie looks like anymore.

Things were so much easier when I was younger. I bet my parents would laugh at me for saying that, because in their mind I'm still too young to have real emotions and thoughts and feelings, too young to have a mind of my own. I don't think it's because they're such bad parents — I think it's because like a lot of grown-ups, they just can't remember how it feels to be a teenager. It's not that our emotions aren't real, it's more that they're hyper-real because we're feeling them for the first time.

I've experienced minor jealousies and hurts before — like pretty much anyone who has survived middle school — but what happened with Matt is so far beyond that I can't help wondering: Does it get any easier? Is the pain of the third, or fourth, or the twenty-fifth betrayal less overwhelming than the first? I sure as hell hope so, because otherwise I'm not sure I want to go on living. There are just so many ways a person you like can hurt you.

There's one immediate benefit from Helen being carted off to the hospital — the Starvers aren't as organized in their mealtime insurrection, so we actually get to eat on time, or at least a lot closer to it. I wonder if someone else will take over as the Starver-in-Chief. Do you think they have an election or draw straws or something? *Vote for me, and I guarantee that those Barfers will have to wait till kingdom come before they get to eat! Elect me and I'll share all my Secret Starver Strategies for Avoiding Calorie Consumption!*

Nah. Even the Starvers can't be that crazy. Or can they? You never know in this place.

Even though it's a little more relaxing at mealtimes without the Barfers chomping at the bit to eat while the nurses play hide-and-seek with Helen, I can't help wondering how she is and if she's going to be okay. I also find I'm spending more and more time thinking about how I can sneak off to purge. I've already managed it once so far today by taking a leaf out of the Starver Book of Stealth and "forgetting" my journal in my room, then quickly puking into a sock and throwing it out the window before heading back to the dayroom to write.

I'm busy finishing up my journal entry before group starts when Nurse Kay walks in with — I can't believe it — another guy. It's just raining men (well, okay, *boys*) here in Golden Slopes. This guy looks about my age, give or take a year, and I'll bet anything he's a total jock — partly because he's wearing a Mattawan High T-shirt, and partly because underneath the T-shirt you can tell he's really buff and his arms are muscled to the point of Popeye. I figure he must be one of the generally screwed-up types, not a Barfer or a Starver. But then Nurse Kay introduces him.

"Janie, this is Royce," she says. "He's a new patient, who will be joining you for Dr. Pardy's group."

She turns to Jock Guy. "Dr. Pardy and the rest of your group will be here in about five minutes. Make yourself comfortable."

Royce sprawls on the sofa and puts his hands behind his head. I wonder if he does it on purpose to show off his bulging biceps.

"What're you staring at?"

I guess I just can't believe that Mr. Mattawan High is an ED patient. He looks too — I don't know — *healthy* to be one of us.

"Nothing, really," I say. "I'm just wondering why you're in here."

He crosses his arms across his chest. "Probably the same reason as you," he says.

"What, you make yourself puke?"

"No, not that," Royce replies. "I just . . . well, I have to make weight for wrestling, see, so before a match I don't eat hardly anything."

"Oh, so you're a Starver," I say. "But you don't look skinny enough to be a Starver." I suddenly realize he might take that the wrong way. "Not that I think you're fat or anything."

"Nah, I'm not fat. My body fat percentage is only seven point five percent."

Well, excuuuuuuuuuuuuuuuuse me, Jock Man. I have no idea what *my* body fat percentage is. Probably like 150 million or something.

"So then what's your problem? I mean, eating-wise?"

"Well, I don't eat to make weight, but then I pig out and eat everything in sight after a match," he says. "Like for a few days, you know, to treat myself for making weight. Then I stop eating again before the next match."

"So you're like . . . I don't know . . . a Binge–Starver or something," I say.

"I don't know what I am," Royce says. "I didn't think there was anything the matter with what I do. It's what lots of wrestlers do. What's the big deal?"

It's weird. When he says that, it's almost like I'm listening to me. But for some reason when I hear it coming out of someone else's mouth it sounds . . . well, maybe not *wrong*, but definitely not *right*.

I'm saved from having to say anything when Tom and Callie join us.

"Guess what, Tommy!" I exclaim. "You're not the only Y chromosome on the block anymore. Meet Royce. He's a hybrid model — a Binge–Starver, minus the puking."

"Hey, Royce," Callie says.

Royce takes in the nose ring and the tattoo and it's clear from his face he disapproves. What a jerk! I mean, I know Callie looks kind of intimidating — she scared the crud out of me when I first met her. But underneath all the piercings and the tattoos, she's actually okay. Well, not as in *okay* okay. Of all the people I've met in here, Callie's the one with the most visible mental armor. But still — it pisses me off that Royce is writing her off just because she doesn't look like some picture-perfect girl. I'll bet he's one of those really traditional uptight chauvinistic-type guys who calls his girlfriend "baby" and expects her to dote on his every word and come to every match to cheer him on, even if she has important stuff to do in her own life.

"Hey, Royce," Tom says. "What's up?"

"Not a whole lot."

I glance over at Royce, because he sounds, I don't know — kind of uptight all of a sudden, even more uptight than I'd expect an uptight Male Chauvinist Pig Super Jock to sound. I'd have thought he'd be more relaxed now that he knows he's not the only dude in the place.

"Oh. My. God! It's . . . a *GUY*!"

You can count on Missy to state the obvious — and loudly, too. She flings herself onto the sofa next to Royce.

"What am I, chopped liver?" Tom jokes.

"Well, I meant a REAL guy . . ." Missy says, leaning closer to Royce and looking at him from under her pale, blond lashes. Next thing you know she'll be batting them at the dude. If she does, I swear I'll puke.

I feel this unexplainable defensiveness for Tom.

"What the hell is THAT supposed to mean?!"

Missy doesn't even turn to look, she's so busy eyeing Royce's biceps and broad chest. *Jeez, have some respect for yourself, girl!* I feel like saying — but I don't.

"You know."

"No, I *don't* know," I say. "Maybe you should explain."

"Forget it, Janie," Tom says.

"No, I . . ."

Despite the fact that I'm seething with anger, I don't get to say anything more because Dr. Pardy walks in.

As usual, she makes the new guy introduce himself first. Royce tells everyone else the same stuff he told me, including bragging about his seven point five percent body fat, a statistic that probably makes the Starver Girls green with envy. I don't know if it's because Missy is looking at him like she wants to eat him for lunch, but he also makes a point of saying how it was his girlfriend (ha! that'll teach Missy) who told his wrestling coach that his star wrestler had a problem. Turns out, the girlfriend was an ED person, too, once upon a time. Guess it takes one to know one. It's clear Royce is still mad at her for helping to make him the unlucky winner of a one-way ticket to Camp Golden Slopes.

"And like I said, I don't have a problem," he sums up. "This is just what wrestlers do to make weight. Everyone does it."

Dr. Pardy has been taking notes on her clipboard, but now she looks around the group. It's obvious that Royce has just earned himself a nice long "vacation" in Eating Disorder Hell.

"What does the group think about Royce's statement? Is his eating behavior a reasonable strategy for making weight?" She leans forward to make her point. "Is it true that 'everyone does it'?"

"No, it's just us — we're the Few, the Proud . . . the Fundamentally Incapable of Having a Normal Relationship with Food," jokes Callie.

"That's not true," argues Bethany, who has become known as the "Niblet" since the peas-in-her-sock incident. Missy was all for calling her the Jolly Green Giant, but since she's short and probably weighs less than a bag of tender green peas flash frozen at the point of picking, the Niblet seemed more appropriate. "There are tons of pro-ana groups on sites like MySpace and Facebook — Web sites, too. So it's not just us."

Pro-ana is like Starvers Anonymous for people who don't want to get better and actually think that looking like a famine victim from the African subcontinent is a *good* thing. They post pictures of the latest Hollywood actresses the tabloids accuse of being anorexic ("New *insert actress's name* Anorexia Shocker!" complete with paparazzi shots of *insert actress's name* in a bikini, ribs countable, face gaunt behind a pair of oversize sunglasses, and legs like toothpicks stuck into a pair of expensive designer slides) and compare notes on how to survive the day on a grape and a prayer.

I think about the time I thought I was alone in the bathroom at school before play rehearsal a few months ago. One of the senior guys on tech crew, Mike Dillard, went out and got a few boxes of Dunkin' Donuts, and before I knew it, even though I'd meant to just have half of one chocolate glazed because I'd only had a few carrot sticks for lunch and I was hungry, I'd inhaled the entire chocolate glazed, plus a chocolate frosted and a sugar jelly, washed down with a Diet Coke.

Of course, the minute I stopped inhaling donuts, I wished I hadn't eaten. I felt disgustingly fat, like I needed a wheelbarrow to carry my bloated stomach around. *You're so gross. You've got no self-control. You suck at being thin and you're going to suck as an actress. People will laugh at you and call you a loser for thinking that you can play the part of Anne Frank when you're really only suited for playing Moby Dick . . .* and so on.

I knew that I'd never be able to concentrate on my lines if I didn't purge, that I would indeed be a Great Fat Failure if I let those calories stay inside me, racing their way through my bloodstream to find a permanent home on my thighs or my butt, my stomach or my hips. So I raced for the bathroom before warm-ups and thanked my lucky stars that it was empty. The second I hit the stall I flipped up the toilet seat and stuck my finger down my throat. At least donuts don't hurt coming up the way things like steak and curry and chili do. I was so busy trying to make sure I'd puked up every last crumb that I didn't realize someone had come into the bathroom.

I almost screamed when I opened the stall door and saw Nancy O'Connell, a junior who was playing Anne's sister, Margot, standing by the sink, her arms crossed and a faint smile on her face. Thinking on my feet, I said, "I think I must be coming down with that stomach bug."

"Yeah, right!" she laughed. "Tell me another one. I know another bulimic when I see one."

"You are SO wrong!" I protested, washing my hands and splashing my overheated face with cold water so my blushing didn't give the lie away.

"Whatever you say, Janie," she smirked. "But if you'll excuse me, I've got to ditch these donuts before rehearsal starts."

She sauntered into one of the stalls and, without even bothering to lock the door behind her, stuck her finger down her throat. I heard the sounds of her retching and then the splatter of regurgitated donuts hitting water. My stomach heaved as I made my escape.

My head was spinning. Here I'd thought I was the only one at school with a dirty little secret. Here I'd been feeling ashamed, like every time I binged and purged was another example of my failure. Yet Nancy seemed completely unashamed, almost *proud* of what she was doing.

After that, Nancy and I became Purge Partners. We'd cover the bathroom door and take turns purging before rehearsal. It's strange — we'd never been all that close despite being in the Pine Hill Players together for the last two years, but now it was like we were sisters in more than just the play, because we shared a secret Bond of Barferhood.

There was no way I could talk to Kelsey about my purging, despite her being my best friend, because I knew she wouldn't approve, and she'd start going on at me about all the dangers and *blah blah blah blah*. Not only that, I was afraid she'd tell her mom, who would then tell *my* mom, and then I'd be *royally* screwed. But keeping this thing that had become such a huge part of my life (if not the main part of my life) a secret from Kelsey made me feel disloyal and unutterably lonely. So it was a relief to be able to share it with Nancy — I felt less isolated, less of a freak.

"Maybe everyone doesn't do it," I tell the group. "But . . . well, it sure *feels* like everyone does . . ."

I stop, cursing myself internally, because I see Dr. Pardy's pen moving across her notepad. Why'd I speak? I resolve to keep my big fat trap shut for the rest of group . . . possibly even the rest of my life.

But it's too late. Dr. Pardy is there with her emotional fishing hook and she's casting it into my troubled waters.

"What makes you feel like everyone does, Janie?"

I can feel everyone looking at me. I wish I could dig a hole in the linoleum and bury myself from view.

"I don't know."

"Sure ya do, sister, or you wouldn't have said it," says Missy. "Spill."

I shoot her a dirty look, but she just grins back, her big blue eyes opened wide with false innocence. I hate her.

Reluctantly, I tell them about Nancy. But I also tell them the endless conversations I've been party to in the cafeteria, where girls have talked about different diets and the caloric content of every single thing on the table. One girl stole her mom's diet pills and another took a trip into Manhattan with her mother to see some Park Avenue "Fat Doctor" who actually prescribed them for her.

"And the freaky thing is, this girl isn't even *fat*," I tell them. "She has a great figure. I'd give anything to look like her."

"Well maybe she has a great figure because she's taking the diet pills," says Tinka, from the Starver corner. "Maybe without them she *would* be fat."

"I suspect that the obsession with weight in that girl's case has more to do with the mother than the daughter," interjects Dr. Pardy. "Unfortunately, it will soon become the daughter's problem, if it hasn't already."

She puts her pen down on her notepad and leans forward, looking around the group.

"You'll read a lot about how the media are responsible for the growth of eating disorders in young people," she says. "And it certainly plays a role. Research shows that women who look at advertisements featuring thin, beautiful women experience greater dissatisfaction with their bodies *and* increased symptoms of depression after looking at them for less than three minutes."

Wow. *Less than three minutes.* I swear I'm never going to look at another fashion magazine again. Or watch TV. Or look at billboards or buses or go see movies or watch videos. Damn. I'm just going to have to walk around with my eyes closed for the rest of my life. But maybe I can open them just a little to peek at the Calvin Klein Underwear for Men ads....

Dr. Pardy pauses and picks up her pen. Note to self: *Keep. Mouth. Shut.*

"But family is equally important — because we get our first cues about attitudes toward weight and food from our families. How many of you would say food or body image is an issue for one or both of your parents?"

I keep my mouth shut, but I raise my hand. Every hand is raised, except for Tracey's — including, surprise of all surprises, Royce Jockstrap.

"So most of you — practically all of you — have grown up with at least one parent who has issues around food. Let's hear about some of them," says Dr. Pardy. "Royce, why don't you start?"

"That's all right. Let someone else go first," he mumbles. I guess he feels like he's been on the Seat of Heat enough for one day.

"Okay, Royce. Just feel free to speak up when you feel comfortable doing so. How about you, Bethany?"

"I think my mom could be anorexic if she wanted to

be. She's pretty anal about what she eats — like she'll count the number of cherry tomatoes she puts in the salad, and I don't think I've *ever* seen her eat dessert or candy," Bethany says.

She starts to tear up, and Tinka hands her the tissue box.

"When I was a little kid, I used to wish I had the kind of mom who baked cookies and let me lick the batter. The kind of mom who would let me have butter on my popcorn at the movies, or even buy me some Twizzlers . . ."

I try to imagine going to the movies *without* Twizzlers or buttered popcorn. My dad even gets extra butter — unless Mom's with us, because otherwise she lectures him about his cholesterol.

"When I first started to lose weight, Mom complimented me every time I lost another pound," Bethany continues. "I liked the praise, and so I started to eat less and less. It was like a competition."

"Was your mother trying to lose weight, too?" asks Dr. Pardy, gently.

"My mother is *always* trying to lose weight. Or she's talking about losing weight, or saying who else needs to lose weight . . . or who looks good because they've just lost some weight," Bethany tells her. "So when she started saying how I was losing too *much* weight, I knew it was just . . . because she was jealous."

"Or *not*," snorts Callie. "Maybe she just didn't want her daughter to end up looking like a famine victim."

Way to go, Callie! That's exactly what I was thinking, but would never dare say.

"What I think Callie is trying to say, although I think she does need to try to express herself in a more constructive way," says Dr. Pardy, throwing a chastising glance in Callie's direction, "is that it's more likely your mother was concerned about your health and well-being than she was jealous."

Bethany isn't convinced.

"Yeah, right. You just don't know her the way I do."

"Well, my mother was jealous, too," Missy says. "Jealous of the way my creep of a stepfather kept looking at me when I wore shorts or a bikini, and that's why she likes it that I got fat. Even though she keeps telling me that I'll never catch the eye of some rich handsome guy if I don't get my figure back. Right. Like I really want to find some pervert who just happens to be loaded like the guy *she* married. I'd rather die."

My mouth opens before my brain can stop it.

"So wait — you mean you weren't overweight before your mom married the Step-Creep?"

"Quick! Give Sherlock Holmes a medal for solving the mystery!" exclaims Callie.

What the heck is her problem? I give her a dirty look.

"I'm just trying to *understand*, Callie. Is that such a crime?"

"Well, you got it in one," says Missy. "El Creepo always insists that we eat together 'as a family' — like he's my family or something. As if! He's just the guy my mother sleeps with, as far as I'm concerned. I can't stand being with him, so I just shovel the food in as fast as I can so I can leave the table and then go purge it back up."

She gives a bitter laugh and grabs a roll of flab that sits above the waistline of her jeans. "There's one advantage of being El Flabulous, though . . . at least now he just makes snide comments about how I look instead of looking at me like he wants to . . . jump me."

I try to imagine how it must feel when your stepfather is looking at you like . . . like *that* and you have to live in the same house. It makes me feel sick. No wonder Missy pukes.

Then Royce surprises us all by speaking up. Voluntarily, the poor, naïve fool.

"My dad is really fitness conscious," he says. "He works out every day. I mean considering he's in his early fifties, he's in damn fine shape. His body fat percentage is like that of a guy five to ten years younger."

I can't help wondering if Royce and his dad sit at the dinner table talking about their body fat percentages the way another family might discuss the day's happenings at school or in the stock market. It makes my family seem almost normal, and believe me, that takes some doing.

"So I think it's cool that my dad's in such great shape and all. But the thing is, he's always giving my mother grief because she could lose a few pounds. I mean, it's not like she's fat. Seriously, Mom's really pretty. But she's had three kids and she's in her forties and she doesn't have the time to exercise every day because she works and has to do everything around the house."

"She should watch out," Tracey says. "Because if her husband is unhappy with her weight and she doesn't do something about it, then she could end up like me. Alone. Ditched for someone younger and thinner."

Ouch.

"Why can't he just love her the way she is?" I wonder aloud before I remember to stop myself.

Callie snorts. "Yeah, right. Maybe in some parallel universe."

"The thing I hate is whenever we go out to dinner and Mom wants to order dessert, Dad asks her if she 'really needs it' or lets her know in some other way that he disapproves," Royce says. "Sometimes they fight, and Mom will say something nasty, like she really *does* need it because she's married to such a jerk."

I can't help thinking Ole Ma Jockstrap has a point.

"But other times, she just gets really quiet and sad and I wish he would just let her have her damn apple pie with vanilla ice cream or chocolate mousse cake or whatever. I mean, what's the big deal if she wears a size ten instead of a size six like she did when they got married? She's a good wife and a great mom. Why does he always have to get on her case?"

You know it's strange, but I'm getting the impression that Royce is actually pretty sensitive for a guy who brags about his body fat percentage within minutes of meeting you. Guess I shouldn't judge a jock by his cover. After all, everyone has a cover in this place. And I'm beginning to see that underneath we're just a bunch of hurting pups, each and every one of us.

"I know just how your mom feels," pipes up Tinka. "I'll never forget the day when my dad told me I was getting chunky. It was a week before I turned fourteen. He'd taken me shopping in Manhattan for my birthday present. It was supposed to be our special Dad and Daughter Day, and I'd been looking forward to it for weeks."

Bethany hands Tinka back the box of tissues because now Tinka's the one who's getting watery eyed. I swear it's like Niagara freakin' Falls in this place today.

"We were in Abercrombie and I tried on a pair of low rider jeans and this really cute cropped T-shirt. When I came out of the dressing room to give Dad a twirl, he said, 'You'd better watch it with the cookies, Tinks. You're getting a little chunky around the ass.'"

What was the guy *thinking*? Sometimes parents can be complete and utter morons.

"To make things worse, there was a really cute guy sitting near Dad waiting for his girlfriend to come out, and he started cracking up. It made me wish I were dead, especially when I saw the guy's girlfriend and she was really thin and gorgeous."

She blows her nose loudly and grabs a few more tissues.

"Why the hell do people have kids if they're going to be so mean to them?" she asks.

"The problem is that parents are only human, and so they can be as thoughtless as the next person," Dr. Pardy answers carefully. "Most parents don't *intend* to be cruel to their children. But people — and I include teachers, coaches, friends, relatives, not just parents in this — can be extremely hurtful without even meaning to, because they speak first and think afterward."

No one speaks after that. I think we're afraid to hurt with thoughtless words, especially witnessing the depth of Tinka's pain, all because her dad couldn't keep his trap shut. Well, he got what he wanted because there's no way Tinka's ass is chunky now. It's bony, almost skeletal, just like the rest of her.

Tom, who has just been observing the whole time without saying a word, speaks up suddenly.

"My mother binges and . . ."

He stops just as suddenly, as if he's just betrayed a state secret, which I suppose he has, if you figure his family is the emotional landscape that formed him; because for all of us, our family is the country we inhabit. *Up against the wall, Tom, my friend. Would you like a blindfold and a cigarette?*

I notice that Royce actually looks at Tom, something he hasn't done the whole time except for the initial cursory glance when Tom came into the dayroom and Royce took an instant dislike to him.

"Have you caught her at it, Tom?" asks Dr. Pardy.

"Not directly. I mean, I've never confronted her about it. But there've been times when I can't sleep and I go downstairs and I see her eating directly from the ice-cream container. Then the next morning I'll find it empty in the garbage, even though it was full the night before."

Dr. Pardy's pen has been scribbling fast.

"That must be difficult for you — knowing your mother is doing something unhealthy and not being able to talk to her about it."

Tom nods.

"I don't get how you're so sure that she's bingeing. Couldn't she have maybe shared the ice cream with your dad or something?" Bethany asks.

Tom gives a short, angry laugh. "Ha! Well, that's highly unlikely, because it usually happens when he's out late. At work or something."

Given what Tom told me, I feel pretty sure it's the "or something," and I wonder if deep down Tom's mom knows that her husband is cheating on her, and Tom just doesn't realize it. However you cut it, I feel sorry for the poor guy. He's a repository of dark family secrets. I bet sometimes he feels like exploding. I wonder how many more secrets he'll spill before Dr. Pardy is done.

I wonder how many she'll be able get out of me.

CHAPTER SIX

July 24th

This morning I asked Nurse Kay how Helen was doing. She wouldn't tell me — patient confidentiality, she said. I think it totally sucks. I always thought it was a good thing to care about what happens to people, not some kind of federal crime. I can't help thinking about Helen and hoping that she's okay. The least they could do is give us an update once in a while.

Mom and Dad came to visit last night. Mom was all sad and pathetic again. It made me wish she had just stayed home. I mean, you'd think she was the one locked up with the Eating Police and Pee-dar, instead of playing doubles at the Club and lying to all her tennis friends about What Janie Is Doing on Her Summer Vacation. It pisses me off because when Mom comes, I become the support-ing actress in The Janie Ryman Story; *what I think and feel takes second place to the drama unfolding on Mom's stage.*

So there's Mom tearing daintily into her designer hankie, while Dad is giving me the Spanish Inquisition about what, exactly, these lying medical crooks are charging him the $500-a-day co-pay for.

"What do you mean you just talk? Isn't there anything else they're doing?"

I think he secretly hopes they can give me some kind of magic pill that will turn me back into his little Pussycat, which I find pretty ironic considering he hates taking even so much as an aspirin. If only it were that easy. I don't think the meds they've got me on are doing anything at all.

Anyway, I tell him about art therapy, where we were asked to draw a personal mandala. In the middle we were supposed to put the things that were at the essential core of ourselves, like the things we feel are the most important to us, and then gradually work our way outward to the things that are least important but still are something to do with who we are.

I found it really hard. I didn't know what to put in the middle, because when I think about who I am, it's a black hole. It's almost as if I can only see myself through the eyes of others, instead of feeling who I am from the inside. So I started to draw the black hole at the middle of my mandala. But then I worried that it would make them think that I'm totally messed up, so I put a yellow question mark on a black background. It's honest, and it's got to be viewed better than a black hole by the Powers That Be.

But you know what's so screwed up about it all? When I told Dad about the mandala, neither he nor my mother asked me what I drew. Mom was too busy sniffing and Dad just went off on a rant about how he was paying all this money for me to draw pictures. "What is this, nursery school?" was one of his choice comments.

I didn't bother to tell him that I'm having my first psychodrama group today. It just wasn't worth the hassle.

But I couldn't help wondering — WHY didn't they ask? Do they think they know me so well that they have nothing new to learn? Am I that boring? Or do they just not love me enough to care?

Either way, it makes me feel like one of the little "presents" our dog, Ringo, leaves out in the yard.

Then, just when I thought I couldn't feel worse, they told me that Perfect Jenny and Brad are coming to visit next week when they get back from their honeymoon. That should just be peachy. Jenny can sit there telling me how I ruined her entire wedding and I won't be able to escape. And Brad — who I've always really liked, and who I get along with way better than I do with Perfect Jenny — will look at me with anger and disappointment in his eyes. I think knowing that Brad doesn't like me anymore

may even be worse than getting ripped a new one
by my half sister. I need to go find a sock.

"So what's psychodrama all about?" I ask Callie and Missy as we're doing our no-purge purgatory after breakfast.

They look at each other and start laughing.

"Well . . ." Missy says. "It's like Woodstock meets Broadway meets . . ."

"*One Flew Over the Cuckoo's Nest*," adds Callie.

I'm a pretty imaginative kinda gal, but I'm having a hard time picturing what the hell they're talking about.

Half an hour later, though, I begin to understand. Helene, the psychodrama lady, is like Grandma Hippie Chick. Her gray hair hangs in a braid down her back, reaching practically to the waistband of her Indian-print skirt, and she wears those Birkenstock sandals that I know are comfortable and good for your feet and all, but which just scream "earthy crunchy." She's got really funky earrings, though, and an armful of bangles that jingle when she gesticulates, which is often.

"I notice some new faces here," she says. "Let's go around the circle and introduce ourselves."

We do the Twelve-Steps intro: "Hi, I'm Janie, and I stick my fingers down my throat after I eat" kind of thing.

"Thank you, everyone, and welcome to the group. Have any of our new members ever done psychodrama before?"

I think about some of the rehearsals for *The Diary of Anne Frank*, and, believe me, they got pretty psycho at times, especially the dress rehearsal where one of the tech crew put a rubber iguana on the window ledge of the attic where Peter Van Daan and I were supposed to be staring dreamily out at the stars thinking of what it would be like to be free of the Secret Annex. Instead, we ended up in hysterical laughter. Mr. Holly, the director, went ballistic. I swear I'd play Anne even better if we did the show again, because now I really understand what it feels like to be trapped somewhere, longing to be free on the one hand, but scared to death of what's on the outside on the other.

I don't think any of this is what Helene means by psychodrama.

"Well, I've acted in plays, quite a lot of them in fact, but I haven't done the psycho stuff," I volunteer. I hope this doesn't mean I'm going to have to go first.

"The difference between acting and psychodrama is that when you're acting, you're taking the role of someone else, whereas here we take off the masks we wear every day, the masks that conceal our deepest feelings from the people around us, and keep us from expressing our true emotions."

O-*kay.* I wonder if she's on some kind of trippy flashback from Woodstock or something.

"Yeah, we learn to express our true emotions to a *chair*," Callie says. "Like *that's* going to help us in real life."

The look of annoyance that passes over Helene's features is so brief I wonder if I really saw it. She takes a deep breath and it's like she's determined to be nice to Callie, despite the fact that Callie seems equally determined to get her riled. I really don't know what's up with Callie. I wonder if even *she* knows. I'm kind of worried about her, to tell you the truth. It's like she's this walking storm of pain these days, lashing out at everything and everyone around her.

"Well, Callie, although this might not make sense to you immediately, I think over the long term you'll find that it's been helpful. Or at least that's my sincere hope."

Callie isn't giving an inch. She's got her arms crossed defensively across her chest, and rolls her eyes as if to say, *yeah, right.*

Helene scans the group and her eyes land on Tom.

"Tom. Why don't you tell us a bit about what led up to your decision to come to Golden Slopes?"

Whew! I feel sorry for Tom, but better him than me.

"Uh...it wasn't exactly my decision," Tom says. "It was my doctor's and my parents' — well, my mother in particular. My dad wasn't so into the idea."

"Why was that, do you think?"

Tom flushes.

"Because...well, because he doesn't believe in anorexia — at least for guys. He thinks it's a girl's disease."

I see Royce nodding, and I'm not sure if it's because he can relate or because he thinks anorexia is a girl's disease, too.

"What does the group think? Is anorexia a girl's disease?" Helene asks.

"Yeah, it is," Royce says.

"Well, obviously it's not, because Tom's anorexic," I retort. I don't know why Royce seems to have it in for Tom.

"But more chicks are anorexic than guys," Royce argues.

"That doesn't make it a *chick* disease," I say. I take it back about him being sensitive; he's obviously a typical chauvinist after all.

"Janie is right, Royce," Helene says. "While it's true that the number of women suffering from anorexia is greater than the number of men, the number of men with eating disorders is on the rise."

She surveys the group, which is pretty light on the Y chromosome, so you can sort of understand where Royce is coming from, even if he *is* a complete chauvinist.

"About twenty years ago, there were thought to be ten to fifteen women with anorexia or bulimia for every one man. These days, it's more like one man for every four women with anorexia, and one man for approximately every ten women with bulimia. So, Royce, anorexia isn't a *chick* disease."

Ooooh, Royce. Consider yourself served. I guess Royce's use of the word "chick" offended Helene's hippie women's lib sensibilities.

Helene turns to Tom, who has been sitting staring at the floor and looking really uncomfortable while this whole conversation is going on.

"And, Tom — you are not alone."

Tom's face reignites now that the attention is focused back on him.

"So tell us a bit more about what precipitated your arrival at Golden Slopes," Helene asks him.

"I was training with my dad — you know, for soccer in the fall . . ."

Missy interrupts, "Yeah, the soccer you don't even want to play!"

"Allow Tom to finish, please, Missy," Helene admonishes.

Tom looks like he'd be quite happy for Missy to interrupt some more so he doesn't have to continue, but there's no such luck so he carries on.

"Well, we were down at the track doing wind sprints and it was pretty hot, and I guess I passed out."

He stops as if he's done, but even a psychodrama newbie like me knows there's no way he's getting off *that* easily.

"You wouldn't be put in here just for passing out because it's hot," Tinka says. "There's got to be more to it than that."

"Well, yeah, there is, I guess. Mom was already pretty worried about me — she knew that I wasn't eating a whole lot, especially for someone with the kind of workout schedule Dad keeps me to, and so when Dad brought me home, she insisted on taking me to the doctor. Dad said she was being a typical neurotic mother and over-reacting, but she just ignored him and bundled me in the car."

"And what did the doctor say?" asked Helene.

"After he lifted up my shirt to listen with the stethoscope, he made me get on the scale. Turns out I'd lost twenty-five pounds since my physical last year. So he and my mom had this big talk while I was in the waiting room, and then Dr. Lipton called me in to his office and started asking me all these questions about how I was feeling mentally and stuff. Mom was all teary-eyed and Dr. Lipton said that he thought I was anorexic and I needed inpatient treatment."

He lifts his eyes from the point on the floor where he'd had them fixed through this whole speech and looks straight at Helene.

"And the rest, as they say, is history."

"How did your father react when you got home from the doctor's office?" Helene asks.

Tom opens his mouth to answer but she holds up a hand to stop him.

"Wait — I want you to *be* your father as you tell us about his reaction."

She takes two empty chairs and places them facing each other in the middle of the circle.

"Come sit here, Tom," she says, pointing at one of them.

With extreme reluctance, Tom shuffles over and sits. He looks beyond uncomfortable, and I don't think it's just because his butt is so skinny that it must hurt him to sit on it.

"Who was it who told your father — you or your mother?" Helene asks.

"My mother," Tom says. "With me sitting there, wishing I could be somewhere else."

"Okay, so you are your father, and I'll be your mother telling him," Helene says.

It's a stretch. You really have to use your imagination to think that earthy crunchy Helene with her Indian-print

84

skirt and long gray braid is Tom's slender, blond mom. It's equally a stretch to imagine skinny Tom as his tough, muscular dad.

"I can be both of them," Tom says.

"If you prefer that," Helene says. She's nothing if not accommodating.

Tom takes a deep breath and becomes his mother.

"*Bob, I need to speak to you. We need to speak to you.*"

"*Can't it wait till after the game?*"

"*No, it cannot, Bob. It's important. Please turn off the television. It's about Tom.*"

"*Okay, okay. I just hope they don't score any runs.*"

Tom turns off an imaginary TV with an equally imaginary remote and leans back, looking irritated.

"*So what's so goddamn important it can't wait until after the game?*"

"*I took Tom to see Dr. Lipton this afternoon to have him checked over. Dr. Lipton said that Tom is anorexic and he needs to be admitted to a hospital.*"

"That's ridiculous, Mary," Tom says. Or rather Tom as his dad says. "*Tom just got a little hot doing wind sprints and passed out. He doesn't have anorexia, for chrissake! Only girls get that — and last time I looked, all his tackle was intact.*"

"*But, Bob, he's lost twenty-five pounds since his last physical. Can't you see he's emaciated?*"

"*Mary, you're being your usual overanxious, overreactive self. The kid has just slimmed down from all the training we've been doing for soccer.*"

"*Bob, listen to me, goddammit!*" Tom as his mom

85

says. He's scarily good at being his mother. He's pretty good at being at his dad, too. *"Dr. Lipton said he's anorexic. He needs treatment. In a hospital. Dr. Lipton wants him checked in to Golden Slopes today."*

"Tom, you're not anorexic, are you, son? You don't want to go into some mental hospital — you'll miss soccer practice."

Tom stops and glances over at Helene. "I need to be me now."

"Be whoever you need to be," Helene says.

"Actually, Dad — I don't know, but . . . well . . . I think I might be anorexic. I'm not sure, but . . ."

"What are you, some kind of faggot? That's a girl disease."

Out of the corner of my eye I see Royce smirk. What the hell is his problem? I mean, just because Tom isn't Mr. Mattawan Wrestling Super Jock, it doesn't mean the guy is *gay*. And even if he was, that's no reason to smirk.

Meanwhile, Tom's getting to be like a comic who does all the different people's voices, except Tom's voices aren't funny like a comic's. They're sad. *Really* sad.

"That's it! I've had enough. Tom, go pack a bag!"

Tom stops. "That last one was my mom. As I left the room to go pack, I heard her asking Dad how he dared to call me a faggot. I went upstairs before he answered. I'm not sure if I want to hear the answer anyway."

He gives a short, bitter laugh. And then I understand.

"So there you have it. The sordid story of how Tom Jackson ended up at glorious Golden Slopes."

"That was excellent, Tom," Helene says. "How did you feel when your parents were arguing like that over you?"

"Not so great," Tom says, in what clearly is in the running for Understatement of the Year.

"But what Enquiring Minds REALLY Want to Know is: How did he feel when his dad asked him if he was a faggot?" Callie says.

A deep red flush starts on Tom's cheeks and slowly moves down his neck until he looks like he's the one-man cause of Global Warming.

"I don't know . . . I mean, I hated that my dad was saying that — especially in that tone of voice . . . like, I don't know . . . like . . . to him, being gay is worse than being a serial killer or something."

He sighs and looks at Helene.

"But I've felt like I've been a disappointment for him as long as I can remember. My wind sprints are never fast enough; I can never score enough goals or make enough assists. I feel like Sisyphus most of the time."

"Sissy-who?" says Royce.

What an ignoramus!

"Not *sissy*, you moron," I tell him. "*Sisyphus*. He was this guy in Greek mythology who was sentenced by the gods to roll a huge rock up a steep hill, but whenever he got to the top it would always roll right back down. So when Tom says he feels like Sisyphus, it's because trying to please his father is a no-win proposition."

"That's kind of like how I feel when I try to please *my* parents," Tinka says.

Now that I think about it, it's kind of how *I* feel when it comes to pleasing *my* parents, because I know that no matter how hard I try, I'll never be as good as my sister.

"That's an interesting point Janie's brought up, although next time, I would appreciate it if you would refrain from calling other group members 'moron,'" says Helene.

"Sorry, Royce," I mumble, although to tell the truth, I'm not sorry at all. He deserved it for being mean to Tom.

"Yeah, whatever," he grunts.

"But to get back to Janie's point . . . there are always going to be people in our lives whom it is impossible to please," says Helene. "As much as we want to, it's unlikely that we'll change *their* behavior. Trying to do that really *is* a Sisyphean task. It's the proverbial butting your head against a brick wall."

She looks at Tom, with kind blue eyes. I suddenly think that she must have been really pretty when she was younger. Or maybe it's just that her kindness makes her *seem* prettier.

"And how does it feel when you stop butting your head against a brick wall if you've been doing it for some time?"

"Fucking awesome!" exclaims Missy.

"Numb," calls out Bethany.

Tracey is raising her hand like she's in grade school, despite probably being as old as Helene — if not older.

"Yes, Tracey?"

"It's frightening," Tracey says in a voice so quiet it's hard to hear her.

"Why do you find it frightening?" Helene asks, fixing Tracey with her kindness beam. You can almost see the positive energy arcing from Helene's bright eyes to Tracey's haggard-looking old-crone face.

"Because . . . because I'm so used to the headache, I'm afraid of what it'll be like to not feel it. Because like Bethany says, without the pain I just feel numb. Like there's nothing. Nothing at all."

"Well, we've certainly brought up a lot to think about today," says Helene. "And unfortunately we have to stop now. But I want to leave you with a few ideas, which I'd like you to think about and perhaps explore in your journaling."

She gets up and starts walking around the circle.

"Firstly, we can't force someone else to change their behavior. . . ." She pauses dramatically in front of Tom. "So, for example, if Tom can't change the fact that pleasing his father is a Sisyphean task, then what are his choices?"

"Duh!" exclaims Callie. "He can stop trying to please the bastard."

"That's true," Helene acknowledges. "Or he can choose to continue trying to please his father, but with the full knowledge that it might be a hopeless task. It's all about choices."

"Or maybe Tom stops doing the stuff he's doing just to please his dad, and starts doing things that *he* enjoys," Royce says.

I stare at him, amazed that he's actually saying something constructive where Tom is concerned. I just don't know what to make of this guy. One minute he's a shallow, bigoted jerk and the next minute he's Mr. Sensitive and Perceptive. Which is the real Royce?

"You've all come up with interesting alternatives about how we can handle a difficult person in our lives," Helene says. "In your journal, I'd like you to think how this might relate to your own life, and perhaps we can explore some situations next time."

She smiles at Tom. "Thank you, Tom, for sharing. That cannot have been easy."

"It was fine," Tom mumbles.

But as he and I are walking out of the room, he says, "I feel like a used dishrag. I just want to go to my room and nap."

"Don't even think about it, Tommy-boy," I warn. "It's lunch time. You don't want to incur the Wrath of the Barfers, do you?"

He gives me a wry smile.

"No, it's bad enough to have incurred the wrath of the gods . . . and my dad. I'm not sure which is worse."

Neither am I, Tom. Neither am I.

CHAPTER SEVEN

July 25th

As much as I hate to admit that I can relate to anything Royce says, his observation about how Tom should stop trying to please his dad keeps running through my brain like that annoying ticker at the bottom of cable news shows. I kept zoning out because I was trying to imagine how it would be if I gave up trying to meet everyone's expectations of me all the time. If I said, "Okay, so Jenny has cornered the Perfect Market — what can I do to be different and special?" Tracey was right, though — it's scary. I've spent practically every day of my life worrying how I measure up in Dad's eyes in comparison to Jenny — usually with the knowledge that it's not favorably. Sure, I might feel better if I stopped beating my head up against that particular brick wall . . . but what would be the alternative?

It comes back to the mandala. If I had to put down my essential Janieness in the center, what would it be? If I'm not always trying to impress people — my parents, my friends, Matt Lewis — if I'm not afraid to be myself and don't always feel like I have to keep up this perfect façade, then who am I? It's almost a joke to say I'm afraid to be myself when I don't even know who "myself" really is, isn't it?

Right now, all I can see is the black hole. How do I go about shining the light into that black hole and figuring out what's in there? And what happens if nothing *is there?*

That's what's so terrifying about letting go of bulimia, the thing that's defined me for so long — I'm afraid that without it, I'll crumple into a heap of nothingness on the floor.

But on the other hand, what if letting go is like being unshackled from leg irons that have been weighing you down? What if doing it makes you so light and free that you can fly?

When we're let loose from the dayroom after our post-breakfast no-puke period, I decide to brave the pay phone to call Kelsey.

I keep dropping the quarters when I try to put them in the phone because my hands are shaking. I don't know why I'm so nervous. She's my best friend, isn't she?

I guess I'm scared she's still mad at me for not telling her I was bulimic. The day after Perfect Jenny's wedding — right before I ended up here — Kelsey came over and we had the mother of all fights. I cringe to think about it, even now.

I still had a hangover from sneaking multiple glasses of champagne at the wedding and I was hiding in my room, partly to avoid facing the wrath of my parents and partly because I couldn't imagine ever wanting to show my face in public again.

Kelsey knocked on my bedroom door and came in, despite the fact I'd groaned "Go away!" and dragged the covers over my head. She pulled them down away from my face and said, "Janie, I've got a bone to pick with you."

"Can't you pick it tomorrow?" I said. "I've got a wicked-ass headache, and I'm pretty sure that's the Grim Reaper standing there in the corner waiting for me."

"I'm not surprised you feel like death," Kelsey said. Her voiced lacked even a smidgen of sympathy. "I think the only thing that surprises me is that Jenny didn't murder you for causing such a scene at her wedding."

"*Please* . . . don't remind me."

"Even if Jenny let it slide on account of wanting to jump into the bed of nuptial bliss, I'm surprised Clarissa hasn't been over here to help you across the River Styx."

"Listen, Kels, if you just came over to remind me of all the people who would like to kill me right now, I wish you'd saved yourself the trip. I'm *really* not up for it."

"Actually, reciting the names on the *I Want To Kill Janie* List — and, believe me, I was only getting started — is just the preview. I came over here to tell you why *I'm* so pissed at you."

I took my arm from over my eyes, where it had been lodged to keep out whatever dim sunlight the curtains let in ever since Kelsey stripped the covers back.

"*You're* pissed at me? What the hell are *you* mad at me about?"

For some reason this seemed to piss her off even more. She stood up and started stalking back and forth across the room like a metronome set to *presto*.

"What am *I* pissed about? Hmmmm . . . let me think. . . . Could it be that you threw up chocolate cake puke all over the Azzedine Alaia dress that my mom with *extreme* reluctance agreed to let me borrow to wear to the wedding? Well, yes, I *am* pissed about that, because now Mom won't let me borrow anything out of her incredibly pricey and stylish wardrobe when it's time for the senior prom."

She stomped over to the curtains and yanked them open. Sunlight thrust daggers into my eyeballs, intensifying the throbbing in my head, which in turn set my already queasy stomach roiling.

"Damn, Kels, why'd you have to do that?"

"Why? Because *I'M MAD AT YOU, JANIE!*"

Whoa! Where did *that* come from? Kelsey and I have spatted plenty, like any friends, but she'd never *screamed* at me like that before.

"Okay, okay, you don't have to shout . . ."

"Says WHO? Actually, I DO have to shout. Why? Because I am so damn furious that my *SUPPOSEDLY* BEST FRIEND has been sticking her finger down her throat to make herself PUKE for the last TWO YEARS and she didn't even bother to tell me!!"

I groaned, because each word was like a mortar exploding in my skull. Not just because of the volume — because I knew she was right.

"Look, Kels, I didn't tell you because . . . because I just didn't know how."

Kelsey stopped pacing, stuck her hands on her hips, and rolled her eyes.

"Last I knew, you just opened your mouth and spoke when you wanted to tell me things. Jesus, you didn't have any problem talking my ear off about Matt Lewis after the cast party, did you?"

Ouch. Hearing Matt's name after what had happened the night before, and especially being reminded of how I'd talked constantly about him in that week after the cast party, was like a sucker punch to the stomach. And I was a sucker all right when it came to Matt Lewis.

"I . . . I just . . . I couldn't talk about it with you . . . because, well, because I thought you wouldn't understand."

"*Damn straight* I don't understand! What would possess you to do something so incredibly *stupid*? I mean, Jesus, Janie. *It's dangerous*. You could ruin your teeth and your esophagus. You could *die*."

"Now you're overreacting. There's no way I'm going to die."

Kelsey resumed her staccato steps back and forth across the room.

"Oh *yeah*?! How do you know?" Kelsey stopped and sat on the end of my bed. I felt her hand grip my ankle. "I'm *worried* about you, Janie. Why would you put your

life at risk just because you're trying to lose weight —
especially since you don't even *need* to?"

I put my arm over my eyes, because I didn't want to
see the anger and disappointment on Kelsey's face.

"You wouldn't understand, Kels. You've got such a
perfect body and . . ."

"What are you *talking* about?!" Kelsey burst out,
causing more mortar explosions in my head. "I don't have
a perfect body. There's no such thing as a *perfect body.*"

Easy for *her* to say.

"Well, at least you're not fat like I am, and guys like
you, and . . ."

I stopped because talking about guys liking her
reminded me of what had happened the night before and
I had to swallow, hard, to keep in the sob threatening to
escape.

"Okay, Janie, listen up and listen up good: (*a*) You are
not fat; (*b*) Guys like you and —"

"No, they don't . . ."

"Shut up and listen to me! *They do, too.* Danny, for
one, is *crazy* about you, which you'd know if you weren't
so busy mooning over that asshole Matt Lewis. Seriously,
Janie, I don't understand why you're so down on yourself all the time. You're really pretty and all you do is rag
on how you look. It's getting old — in fact, it's getting
beyond old."

In between drumbeats in my head, all I could think
was that she was just saying I was pretty and not fat
because she didn't want me to lose more weight because
then guys might like me instead of her. I didn't realize

I'd said it aloud until I heard Kels say, "I can't believe after all these years of friendship that's how little you think of me."

Her hand came off my ankle and it sounded like she was crying.

I uncovered my eyes and, yes, she was crying.

"Kels, I'm sorry, I . . ."

She waved her hand to shut me up as she got up and walked toward the door.

"I thought you knew me better than that, Janie. I thought I was your best friend," she said, swiping away tears with the back of her hand. "I guess I was wrong. I just don't know you anymore."

"Kelsey, wait . . ."

But she was gone, slamming the bedroom door behind her. If I felt crummy before Kelsey walked in the door, it was nothing compared to how awful I felt when she left. I don't think I ever felt so alone in my entire life. It was like I'd burned my last bridge to normalcy.

Matt Lewis hates me, Danny hates me, Clarissa hates me (even though that's nothing new), Jenny hates me, Mom and Dad hate me, and now Kelsey hates me, too.

But no matter how much they hated me, it didn't even begin to compare to how much I hated myself.

I finally manage to get the quarters in the pay phone slot and dial Kelsey's number with shaking hands.

Her mom answers.

"Hi, Mrs. Critelli — it's Janie. Is . . . Kelsey there?"

Please let her be there and be willing to speak to me. Please don't let her have written me off. Please don't let my best friend hate me forever.

"Sure, honey. How are you doing?"

I can't believe how kind and caring she sounds, especially since I puked chocolate cake all over her Azzedine Alaia dress and I can't imagine the stains will ever come out, even if they take it to some ultra-expensive specialty dry cleaner.

"Um . . . well, not so good actually. I'm . . . in the hospital . . . for bulimia."

I figure my mom's told her I'm at drama camp or something, so I'm completely floored when she says, "I know, dear. I think it's terrific that you're getting help, I really do."

"Mrs. Critelli, I'm really, *really* sorry about your dress. I promise I'll pay for the dry cleaning and . . ."

"Oh, Janie, don't even think about the dress. I have plenty more in my closet. But there's only one of you, and the main thing is that you look after yourself and get healthy."

I feel a lump start to form in my throat. I wonder if maybe I'll be able to cry again.

"Good luck, sweetie. We're all praying for you. I lit a candle for you in church on Sunday. Anyway, I know you don't want to waste your time listening to me jabber. I'll just call Kelsey — she'll be *thrilled* to be able to speak to you."

I wish I could be so sure. As I'm waiting to see if Kelsey will come to the phone, I'm trying to get over the amazement that my mother actually told Mrs. Critelli the truth instead of some polite fiction for the sake of appearances. It's not like Mom to admit that All Is Not Perfect in the House of Ryman. Not like Mom at all.

"Hey, Janie . . . how're you doing?"

Hallelujah! She's talking to me!

"I'm . . . okay. Well, as okay as I can be in a psychiatric hospital, I guess."

Kelsey laughs, and my heart beats faster at the sound of it. Please let it mean she's forgiven me and is still my friend.

"Kelsey, listen, I'm . . ."

"Sorry. Yeah, I know. So am I."

"What the hell do *you* have to be sorry about? You didn't puke on your best friend's designer dress and ruin your half-sister's dream wedding, disgrace your entire family, and insult your best friend when she came to tell you what a screwup you are."

The silence that follows is a few seconds too long for comfort.

"Well, okay, you've got a point. I couldn't believe what you said to me, Janie. I was . . . well, I don't think I've ever felt so . . . horrible . . . so hurt by someone's words, in my *entire life*."

I feel like pond scum all over again.

"I know, I'm sooo sorry. Seriously, I feel awful and—"

But she cuts off my apologies.

"And it's true — personally, I prefer to *wear* designer dresses instead of *puking* on them. I didn't ruin my half-sister's dream wedding, namely because I don't have a half sister and the only sister I *do* have is only twelve, so she's not getting married anytime soon. I tell you what,

Janie, if it makes you feel better, I can try really hard to ruin her Sweet Sixteen party when the time comes."

One of the reasons I love Kelsey is that she makes me laugh when I'm feeling sorry for myself.

"Nice ... but I really don't want your mom thinking I'm more of a bad influence than she probably does already."

"Puh-leeze," Kelsey says. "You know my mother thinks you walk on water."

"Nuh-uh," I say. "Anyway, Nice Jewish Girls — okay maybe not so nice — like me aren't capable of walking on water. We leave that to *your* guy."

Kelsey laughs. "Seriously, though, Janie — you *did* hurt me. So bad I thought our friendship was over. But after ... what happened ... I realized that I didn't need to come bawl you out the day after the wedding when you were an obvious wreck. It was like kicking a help-less puppy. And you know how strongly I feel about helpless puppies."

Kels is a vegetarian and an active member of our high school's chapter of PETA. She feels pretty strongly about anything to do with animals, let alone helpless puppies.

"Yes, I do know how strongly you feel. And Kels ... I really *am* sorry for what I said."

"Please. Don't mention it again or else you really *will* be sorry. Now spill ... I want to hear all the dirt about what goes on in a psych hospital."

I tell her all about the Barfers and the Starvers, and the stupid rules about mealtimes and how humiliating it is to have to try and perform bodily functions with someone listening outside the door.

"If it were me, I'd be constipated for *weeks*," Kelsey says. "I can't even go at school when there's someone in the next stall."

I finally summon up the courage to ask: "So, Kelsey . . . how's Danny? Have you seen him? Does he hate me?"

She doesn't answer right away, and I feel sick to my stomach. I can't bear to think of Danny hating me. Funnily enough, it bothers me more than the idea of Matt Lewis hating me. I think of Danny's arm catching me, preventing my fall when I tripped onto the dance floor at Jenny's wedding. I remember when we were back in fifth grade and he handed me a bunch of daffodils from his mom's garden the first time I had a part in a play.

I might have worshiped Matt from afar for years, but I've been friends with Danny for even longer.

"I saw him yesterday at the beach. He was asking about you . . . where you've been. He's left a bunch of messages on your voice mail and you haven't responded to his e-mails or when he's texted you. I . . . I didn't know what to tell him. I really wanted to let him know what's going on, but your mom seemed pretty keen that we keep your location top secret. I feel awful. . . . I'm sure he knows that I know what's up and I'm not telling him. You know what an awful liar I am."

Ha! I knew Mom would want to keep this under wraps. She probably only told Mrs. Critelli because otherwise she knew Kelsey would be calling every day to ask where I was.

"What *did* you tell him?"

"I said you were away for a while."

"But did he say anything about that night?"

Kelsey hesitates again.

"C'mon, Kels. *Tell* me. I need to know."

"He's worried about you, Janie. You might not believe it, but Danny really cares about you. So do I. You should call him. Seriously."

"I'll think about it."

And I do, for about a nanosecond, before I know I'm too much of a coward.

"So . . . he really doesn't hate me?"

"Of course he doesn't, you jerk. Danny thinks the world of you, and you know it."

The sense of relief I feel from hearing that Danny doesn't hate me is almost as big as the relief I'm feeling that Kelsey is still my best friend. Almost.

"Kelsey, you're the best. And I know I'm not supposed to say it again, but I really *am* sorry."

Callie appears behind me. "I hate to interrupt this little *lovefest-slash-confession*, but is there any danger of you getting off the phone so I can make a call before group?"

I give her a dirty look.

"Listen, Kels, I have to go. Call me, okay?"

I give her the pay phone number and hang up.

"Why are you being such a bitch, Callie?"

She glares at me as she feeds quarters into the phone and starts dialing.

"It's the only way to get by," she says. "Now shove off and give me some privacy, *please*."

The morning group is a session with Tina, the nutritionist, about "mindful eating." She starts off by asking how many of us eat while watching TV or reading or doing something else.

"We always have the TV on while we're eating," says Bethany. "But I don't mind because it means my mom's not focusing on what I'm eating — or *not* eating, as the case may be."

"I wish I could watch TV instead of having to listen to my asshole stepfather pontificate about everything from who is going to win the World Series to the political situation in Timbuktu, even though he doesn't know squat about either topic," Missy grumbles. "That *alone* is enough to make me want to puke."

I think about my own eating habits. It's one thing when I eat with my family, because we're not allowed to watch TV or read anything during mealtimes. We're supposed to *interact* and have *family discussions*, although basically that means listening to Dad rant about what's going on in the stock market or how a certain politician doesn't know his ass from his elbow, or Mom blathering on about the Wedding, the Wedding, the *goddamn freakin'* Wedding. I wonder what she's going to talk about now. Probably Harry's Bar Mitzvah . . . argh.

But when I'm by myself I can't stand to eat without doing something else at the same time — except when I'm bingeing. Then I don't have time to do much else other than figure out what I'm going to stuff my face with next and how soon I'm going to be able to purge. When it's just normal eating, like breakfast on the weekend after everyone else has already eaten, I've *got* to read. I'll read the cereal box if I have to, but I can't just sit there and look at my food when I eat by myself — no way, no how.

"People with eating disorders tend to try to distract themselves from the act of eating," Tina says. "So today, we're going to focus on what it feels like to be mindful of what we put in our mouths."

She stands up and walks around, handing each person one of those mini snack boxes of raisins.

"I'd like each of you to take out one raisin."

"We're not going to have to eat these, are we?" Tinka says. "Because I'm already on a twenty-five-hundred-calorie-a-meal diet and that's bad enough. Dried fruit is incredibly high in calories, you know."

"Of course she knows, you idiot! She's the *nutritionist*," Callie says.

"*Callie*," Tina warns. "And Tinka, you don't have to eat the whole box. You do, however, have to eat one raisin."

It looks like a mutiny's brewing over on the Starver side of the room. As someone who has consumed an entire tub of Betty Crocker chocolate fudge cake icing washed down with two glasses of milk (even if I did puke it all up immediately afterward), I find it really hard to understand how anyone can get that freaked out by having to eat one itty-bitty raisin. But I guess that's why I'm bulimic and not anorexic.

"First, I would like you to smell the raisin," Tina says.

We all sit there snorting raisins. I'm tempted to stick my raisin up my nose for comic relief because all the Starvers are so seriously freaked out about the whole thing. But I don't.

"Now I'd like you to feel the raisin . . . squeeze it and roll it around between your fingers."

I roll the raisin between my thumb and forefinger. It's squishy and plump within its wrinkled outer skin.

"And now I'd like you all to close your eyes and put the raisin in your mouth. Don't bite down on it right away. Just feel the taste of it on your tongue."

The raisin is in my mouth. As I trace the wrinkles with my tongue, I sneak a glance at the Starvers. The grimaces on their faces almost make me crack up and give myself away — they're like the gargoyles on Notre Dame. Shutting my eyes again, I roll the raisin around with my tongue. It's weird — I must have eaten thousands of mini snack boxes of raisins in the course of my life, but I've never been as aware of what a raisin feels like in my mouth as I am right at this very minute.

"Now I want you to bite into your raisin," Tina says.

My teeth pierce the raisin's outer skin and I experience an explosion of sweetness in my mouth — this rush of raisiny flavor that is so intense it's like I never tasted a raisin before. It makes me wonder how I ever managed to throw a handful of the suckers into my mouth at the same time. What a waste of amazing flavor! From now on, I'm going to eat my raisins one at a time.

"Okay, everyone, you can open your eyes now, and we'll talk about how that experience was for you."

"Can I spit this out?" Tinka whines. "I really don't want to finish it."

"Can I finish my box of raisins?" Missy asks. "In fact, I'll have Princess Skinnybutt's, too, since she can't even manage to eat ONE FREAKING RAISIN without getting ants in her anorexic pants."

"No, you cannot spit it out, Tinka. Missy, you need to focus on your own emotions about this, not on Tinka's," Tina says.

"I am," Missy grumbles. "My emotions are telling me that I want to finish her box of raisins."

"Royce, how was it for you?"

Tina catches him while he's busy emptying the rest of the box of raisins into his mouth, all at once.

"Uh . . . it was okay. It was like . . . eating a raisin."

I guess it wasn't good for him, too. Clearly, one girl's explosion of intense raisiny pleasure is another guy's ho-hum raisin-consumption experience.

"It made me want to throw up," Bethany says. She's practically gagging.

"Ooh, you don't want to go down that road, Niblet," warns Callie.

"Did it make you uncomfortable to have to focus on the act of eating?" Tina asks.

"I felt freaky," says Tinka. "All I could think about was the calories."

"Let's look at that for a minute," Tina says. "There are forty-five calories in this box of raisins, and let's say there are about twenty-five raisins in the box. So one raisin — the one raisin I've just asked you to eat, is just under two calories."

"Yeah, but if you're only allowing yourself like twenty calories a day like Niblet and the rest of the Twiglets, that's like ten percent of your recommended daily allowance," says Missy. "So it's no wonder the Starvers are freaking out."

"It made me realize how amazing raisins taste," I say, before I remember my pledge to keep my mouth shut.

Still, it works out. I figure I'll get a few points in the sanity column because Tina smiles and says, "Yes, Janie. One of the purposes of this exercise is to get us to really focus on our food, instead of trying to distract ourselves from the fact that we're eating."

She looks at those of us on the Barfer side of the room.

"When you are bingeing, how aware are you of what you're eating?"

Missy laughs. "I don't care what I'm eating as long as it's sweet. It's like I'm in this eating frenzy when I binge — all I care about is eating. I can eat an entire thing of that ready-to-bake cookie dough . . . like in less than sixty seconds, as long as I have a glass of milk to wash it down."

By the horrified looks on their faces, I can tell the Starvers have already worked out the caloric content of a log of cookie dough and a cup of milk.

"Yeah, it's not till afterward that I think about what I've eaten — and then all I can think about is how quickly I can get to a bathroom and get it out," Callie adds.

"Even people who don't have eating disorders are guilty of eating in a non-mindful way," says Tina. "I find that my non-ED clients who want to lose weight have been able to do so by practicing mindful eating, rather than eating in the car or while reading or watching TV."

I'm wondering how this plays out for the Starvers. I

mean, they want to lose more weight even if they don't need to, but clearly it's hell for them to have to concentrate on their food.

"I'd like you all to practice mindful eating at all of your meals for the next two days. Write about your feelings in your journals and we can discuss things further next time."

As we're walking out of the dayroom, I ask Tom about his raisin-eating experience.

"Was it good for you, too?"

He laughs.

"Obviously it wasn't as good for me as it was for you. I thought you were going to start doing porn movie moans in the middle of group." He closes his eyes: "*Yes, baby, oh YES, give me your fat, juicy, luscious . . . raisins!*"

"*Voulez-vous manger avec moi, ce soir?*" I sing. "*Voulez-vous manger avec moi . . . .*"

"You guys are sick," says Bethany as she walks by — but she's smiling, something I haven't seen her do the entire time I've been here.

This is progress, I suppose.

CHAPTER EIGHT

July 27th

Still no word about Helen. I tried asking Nurse Joe this time, but he gave me the same line about "preserving patient confidentiality." Why can't they just tell me if she's doing better, to put me out of my misery?

Meanwhile, I swear this place is turning more Zen by the day. First we had the mindful raisin-eating thing yesterday morning, then in the afternoon we had yoga. "At Golden Slopes we are firm believers in exercise as part of the mind-body connection," according to Ali, the yoga instructor. That's only partly true, because if you're a Starver, you aren't allowed to do any exercise at all. In fact, if you're a Starver, you're practically ordered to be a couch potato. It would almost be worth becoming a Starver in order to get a permanent pass to miss gym. The only drawback would be the part about not being able to eat anything.

Ali, the yoga instructor, is like a human pretzel. I don't know how she manages to bend herself into those positions and still be able to take deep breaths while she's doing it. I could barely breathe at all, much less take deep, cleansing breaths to the count of four.

At the end she had us lying on the floor on mats with our eyes closed to do this meditation exercise where we were supposed to empty our brain of all thoughts.

"That won't be hard for some people," Callie whispered, nodding meaningfully in Royce's direction.

I started cracking up, which didn't do a whole lot for my "mindfulness." I found it really hard to empty my brain, which I suppose is good in some ways because it means I have a lot in it, but it also means that I'm pretty much a failure at yoga. Every time I tried to think emptiness, stuff would just pop into my head.

"Relax and feel your body melt into the mat," Ali said in this mesmerizing voice.

Ha! That's part of my problem. I already let my body melt into the Matt.

It's really weird how your brain will take you from one thought to the next on this strange, uncharted road, but no matter where you start out or which path you decided to take you always seem to end up back at the one thing you really don't want to think about. Like I started off with a chuckle remembering what Callie said about Royce and that led to thinking about drama people like me versus jocks like him and that led me to when I played the lead in Anne Frank a week before the wedding and how I got a standing ovation. Then I found myself thinking about the cast party and how I was talking to Danny and Kelsey when in walks Matt Lewis, on whom I've had the biggest crush ever since back in middle school when his parents invited my family to their country club for drinks and tennis. (His dad is one of my dad's hedge fund clients.) For once, Stage Janie merged with Real Janie and I was actually able to flirt with him instead of just standing there blushing and barely able to stammer out a sentence. We ended up making out in one of the bedrooms of Kenny Dillard's house, and it felt amazing to be going at it with the guy I'd dreamed about for so long. And then I started remembering how it felt to be sitting at the head table at Perfect Jenny's wedding next to Brad's deathly boring cousin from Ohio and seeing . . . oh, G-d, I don't want to go there.

So I started from the beginning, focusing on my breath and trying to imagine myself in a safe, warm place. The stage, with the warmth of the spot-lights shining down on me, hiding the audience from sight. The stage, where I can be anyone I want to be. The stage, where I felt so happy the night of the Anne Frank performance and . . . no, can't go there, either.

I took another deep cleansing breath and tried again. Okay, a beach. A beach, under a sapphire sky, *the sun warming my skin. But being on a beach means I'm in a bathing suit. Is my stomach hanging out? Is everyone thinking how fat and ugly I look?*

You get the picture. There are times when I wish more than anything that I could turn off my brain, turn off that constantly critical voice inside, turn off the memories of that night. But instead, I guess I just have to add yoga and meditation to the list of things I suck at.

"Hey, Janie, get your ass into the dayroom. You've got visitors," Callie shouts from outside my door.

Visitors? I thought Mom and Dad said they weren't coming tonight because Dad has a business meeting and Harry has a baseball game or something. Actually I think Mom made up the baseball game because she can't hack the thought of visiting me by herself without Dad. Anyway, I don't care — it's a relief not to have to put up with her crying. I'm sick of having to be the comfort*er* instead of the comfort*ed*.

But I can't imagine who might be waiting for me in the dayroom. *I hope it's Kelsey and Mrs. Critelli*, I think as I hurry down the hallway.

No such luck. My heart sinks as I walk into the dayroom and see none other than Perfect Jenny, sitting stiffly on the couch next to a somewhat more relaxed Brad. Not that being more relaxed than Jenny is much of an accomplishment — even an ice sculpture would look warm and relaxed next to her.

Brad spots me first and I see him giving Jenny's hand a squeeze. I'm not sure if it's to give her support and encouragement or to warn her not to kill me. Judging by the expression on her face when she sees me walking toward her, it's probably the latter.

"Hey, Janie," Brad says with what I assume is forced cheer. "How's my favorite sister-in-law doing?"

"It's okay, Brad. You don't need to pretend I'm your favorite sister-in-law, because I'm your *only* sister-in-law. And if you really want to know how I'm doing, well, I'm doing *completement merde*, thank you very much."

Jenny rolls her eyes.

"I *told* you she would be like this," she says to Brad, as if I'm not there. Then she turns her gaze back to me. "Brad was just trying to be nice. You know, to be civil and respectful. Not that you deserve it, after the way you behaved. You certainly didn't show *us* any respect."

Ouch. It's not like I expected anything different, but still . . . it hurts.

Brad puts a hand on Jenny's shoulder and gives her a warning glance.

"Now, girls — let's try to keep things calm."

One of the things I've always admired about Brad is his relentless optimism, but under the current circumstances I think it qualifies him as delusional. Still, I figure I owe it to him to try to break the ice with his wife. Besides, if I were Jenny, I'd hate me, too. So I take a deep breath and launch in:

"Look, Jenny . . . Brad . . . I really am sorry about what happened. I feel terrible about it. I know how much planning went into making the day . . ."

I hesitate, trying to think of a word other than "perfect."

"To make it . . . special . . . and meaningful . . . and I really think it was, even if I did embarrass you all and everything . . . and . . ."

Damn, this is hard. Jenny's still sitting there like the iceberg that sunk the *Titanic*, her cold hostility ripping a hole in my hull. If only she'd just . . . I don't know, show me some sign that she doesn't completely hate me, or at least that even if she *does* hate me that there's some remote possibility she might not in the future — assuming I grovel long and hard enough, that is.

"Well . . . I guess that what I'm trying to say is . . . that I hope you'll be able to . . . you know . . . *forgive* me eventually and . . . well, I wish I could make it up to you in some way, but I know that I can't."

"Now there's an understatement if I ever heard one," Jenny says. "*I'll* say you can't."

I start to wonder how long I have to stay here listening to her being mad at me. Is there some point where I can just say, "*Enough, already! I've apologized, let's put it behind us and move on*"? Or maybe this is part of the penance — having to put up with being berated for the next, like, twenty years of my life. Oh. Joy.

"I mean, seriously, Janie. You *knew* how important my wedding was to me — because unlike *Dad*, I only plan on getting married *once*."

I guess I'm not the only one Jenny's mad at.

"I can't tell you how happy it makes me to hear that, sweetheart," Brad says, smiling as he puts his arm around Jenny.

Brad might not be the most handsome guy in the world — he's got a kind face and is built a little like an overstuffed teddy bear — but he's definitely got a certain *je ne sais quoi* as far as Jenny is concerned. She actually smiles back at him — I can't help hoping that this little melting of the polar ice cap will extend in *my* direction. I feel seriously bad about ruining her wedding and all, but groveling is getting really old, *really* quickly.

"Jenny, believe it or not, I didn't *set out* to ruin your wedding — even though you made me wear a bridesmaid's dress that resembled a lemon meringue pie. It's just... just that, well, something happened that night that really upset me and... the rest, as they say, is history. And believe me, it's history I'd much rather be forgotten."

I wish I could cry, because I think Jenny might actually believe me if she saw real tears. But the tears won't come. I don't know if it's because of the meds they put me on here or what, but I just can't seem to summon up the ability to cry. Maybe I've used up all my tears.

What makes it worse is that Jenny *does* start to cry, and if I felt bad about things before, seeing her break down makes me feel a gazillion times more awful.

"I just don't understand it. What made you behave that way? Do you hate me that much?" she sobs.

Brad reaches for one of the omnipresent boxes of tissues, and rubs Jenny's back. I hope if I'm ever nuts enough to risk matrimony, I end up with a guy like him. With my luck, though, I'll end up with someone like Tom's dad. Or someone like Royce's dad, who'll constantly tell me how fat I am and how I'm doing everything wrong — as if I don't have enough of that from the voice in my *own* head.

I feel a lump in my throat like I *want* to cry but the tears just won't come.

"I — I don't hate you, Jenny. Really I don't. If anything I . . . *envy* you."

Jenny looks up, her tearstained face registering surprise.

"Why on earth would *you* envy *me*?" she says. "You didn't have to grow up shuttling back and forth between parents who couldn't even speak a civil word to each other, or hearing your mother telling you what a lying, cheating bastard your dad is all the time. Believe me, my life growing up was nothing worth envying."

I guess it *was* really hard for Jenny when Dad and Clarissa split up. It makes me wonder how she can even look Mom in the eye, let alone be friends with her. Maybe Jenny's just good at forgiveness. I sure as hell hope so.

I figure I owe it to her to try to explain why I envy her so much.

"It's just — you're so *perfect*. You're smart and gorgeous and you went to Yale, just like Dad . . . for that *alone* he worships the ground you walk on. It's like you're this ideal daughter that I can never, ever live up to."

I'm taken aback when Brad bursts out laughing. In fact I'm kind of pissed at him. I mean, here I've bared my soul about my lifelong Perfect Jenny Complex and the guy is *laughing*. It's no wonder I'm stuck here in Crazy Castle when I've got family like this to deal with.

"Jenny? *Perfect*?" he says between guffaws. "That's the funniest thing I've ever heard."

Thank you, Brad. You just saved my bacon — because after that comment, Jenny's pissed at *you* instead of me.

"Why, exactly, is that so funny? Boy, the honeymoon really *is* over," she sniffs.

Brad takes her hand and kisses it.

"Darling, even you have to admit you're not perfect. Janie's not perfect and you can bet that I'm not perfect, either — although I have to admit that unlike you two, I come pretty damn close," he says with a grin.

Brad hugs Jenny to him and kisses her temple.

"I love you more *because* of your imperfections, honey. I love the fact that beneath that cool, competent façade there's a woman who fishes all of the brownie out of the Ben & Jerry's Chocolate Fudge Brownie and leaves the ice cream, and who acts like a two-year-old when she sees a spider."

"I don't fish out *all* the brownie," Jenny protests. "Just the clearly visible parts."

"I stand corrected," Brad says, his eyes twinkling. "She just fishes out the clearly visible parts, even if some of them become visible as a result of vigorous exploration with a spoon."

You know, when Jenny first brought him to meet Dad, I was like, *Jenny's so beautiful; she could do better than Brad.* But I'm beginning to see that it would be hard to find someone better. Now that I've gotten to know Brad better, I don't even notice the fact that he doesn't have six-pack abs and he's beginning to bald. He's so funny and kind. And he obviously really loves Jenny.

I know they say you shouldn't judge a book by its cover or a person by their looks. But it seems like ever since, I don't know, fourth grade or so, looks are the only thing we get judged by. Why is that? Why is it that the things we are and the things we do don't seem to count for much?

"Well, brownie excavator or not, Dad certainly doesn't worship the ground I walk on," Jenny says. She turns to Brad, who is stroking her hair. "You, on the other hand, should feel free to worship to your heart's content."

"Are you kidding me?" I say. "Dad totally worships you. I mean, all I ever get is *Jenny did this* and *Jenny did that* and *Jenny graduated summa cum laude from Yale; she's a chip off the old block, that's my girl.*"

Brad laughs. "Janie does a good Hal imitation."

But Jenny's serious. "That's the whole point," she says. "I've always had to *do* things to get Dad's attention."

"Aha! So I have to blame Hal for the fact that you're a relentless overachiever, is that it?" Brad says.

She hits him.

"Can you be serious for a change? This is important."

Jenny turns back to me and actually *takes my hand.*

"Janie, you should hear Dad talking about you. I thought he was going to take out a full-page ad in *The New York Times* when you got the lead in *The Diary of Anne Frank.*"

"But —"

"Seriously, Janie. You have no idea how hard it was for me when you were born. It was bad enough when Dad ditched Mom for Carole — but then when they had you it was like Dad was trying to replace me with a trophy daughter, just like he replaced Mom with a trophy wife."

Her eyes fill with tears again. I've got an ever-growing lump in my throat but the tears *still* won't come.

"It was easier with Harry, because he's a boy and I know that Dad always really wanted a boy. But with you . . . you were this adorable little baby and I was going through this awful time in middle school — it was . . ."

Brad hands her another tissue and she blows her nose, loudly.

"Anyway . . . Dad doesn't worship *me* any more than he worships *you*."

She looks at me, eyes brimming.

"But I need to know something, Janie. And that's . . . *why*? What made you get drunk and create such a scene at our wedding?"

What do I say? *I ruined your wedding because I realized the guy I'd worshiped from afar for years, who I thought cared about me, turned out to be a complete jerk? I hurt you because I was hurting myself?*

"I . . . well . . . I was really upset about something."

"What? *Tell me* what you were so upset about. Is it something to do with you wanting to rearrange the seating plans at the last minute so you could sit next to Matt Lewis?"

The mere mention of his name is a blow to the solar plexus. How long does it take for the pain to go away? I want Jenny and Brad to leave, *now*, so I can go to my room and find a sock. I don't want to have to feel this anymore.

"Visiting hours are over," Joe announces from the doorway. "Let's wrap things up, people."

I'm totally loving Nurse Joe right now. But unfortunately, Jenny is still sitting there waiting expectantly for an answer.

"Well . . . yes . . . kind of . . . it does have to do with that," I say. "But it's a long story and visiting hours are over. Let's talk about it when I get out of here."

"Sure thing, Janie," says Brad, getting up from the sofa and extending his hand to help Jenny. "Any idea of when you'll be sprung?"

"No, unfortunately. It's indefinite incarceration with no opportunity for parole."

Jenny is looking like she's got serious unfinished business, but Brad's hustling her toward the door.

"Jenny, Brad, wait!" I take a deep, cleansing breath. "I just want to say again how sorry I am. About the wedding. About everything."

Jenny turns and her eyes are brimming again.

"Thanks, Janie."

She kisses me on the cheek. Brad gives me a bear hug.

"You take care of yourself, kiddo. We need you on the outside." Then he whispers in my ear, "If it gets really bad, call me and I'll smuggle in escape tools in a cake or something."

I actually manage a giggle. Then, as soon as they've left, I go to my room and fill up a sock.

CHAPTER NINE

July 28th

I still can't believe I survived the confrontation with Jenny and lived to tell the tale. But even more, I still can't believe that she ever thought Dad would prefer me to her. It's just so completely unthinkable. Well, I guess it's not completely unthinkable because Jenny thought it. But still. It got me wondering about how differently we all perceive the things that go on in our lives. Like I've spent my whole life feeling like I live in Perfect Jenny's shadow, and meanwhile she's there thinking that I'm Dad's Trophy Daughter. Hahahahahahahaha! The idea is so incredibly laughable, especially given the current circumstances. I bet Dad considers me more of a skeleton in the closet than a trophy these days.

If surviving Jenny's visit in one piece is the good news, the bad news is that ever since last night I've been thinking about Matt constantly and it's like picking at a scab that has barely begun to heal and feeling the pain all over again. Images of the two of us together and then . . . well . . . not together . . . the night of Jenny's wedding, are on this endless loop in my head, and I want, more than anything, for it to stop. I don't want to see it, I don't want to think about it, I don't want to feel it. I wish I could just edit the footage out of my brain or somehow pull the plug on the projector, because then maybe I wouldn't feel the pain in my heart and in my stomach every time one of those pictures flashes up.

I keep asking myself why I'm so hung up on Matt Lewis when he behaved like such an asshole. For one thing, it's not easy to forget how gorgeous he is, like something out of an Abercrombie catalog, with his athlete's body and the blond hair that flops over one eye. I crushed on him, instantly, the first time I met him at his parents' country club. We ended up playing doubles, him and me against Harry and Matt's older brother, Ben. The way Matt moved on the court was amazing, more than making up for my deficiencies with a racket. When we beat Harry and Ben, he didn't just high-five me; he picked me up and spun me around. Just looking at him over lunch on the patio afterward, while our parents toasted the stock market with mimosas, was enough to give me butterflies.

The thing is, Matt isn't just gorgeous — he's smart and funny, too. You know how some people seem to have hit the genetic jackpot? Matt's one of those people who have it all and you can either hate them for it or fall madly in love with them. I, unfortunately, did the latter, fool that I am.

So I've basically been worshipping the guy ever since the summer between seventh and eighth grade. I didn't see him so much in eighth grade because he went to a different school, but both middle schools feed into Pine Ridge High, so in ninth grade I started seeing him on a daily basis. We were even in a bunch of honors classes together.

In a way, though, it was harder to see him more often, because it meant I also had to experience the Mattettes — the posse of groupies that follow the guy like a flock of overeager ducklings everywhere and anywhere he goes.

How could I have ever thought that someone like Matt would really want someone like me to be his girlfriend? I should have my head examined. . . . Oh, wait, I'm in a psych ward. So I guess I am having my head examined. Sigh . . . Not that it seems to be doing me a whole lot of good. I want to get out of here. I want to be back at home. I miss my dog and my room and my comfortable bed and my sheets that smell like fabric softener instead of bleach. I miss my iPod and my cell phone and being able to choose what to watch on TV. I miss being with my friends and being able to talk without being afraid that someone will write down everything I say. Most especially I miss being able to perform bodily functions without an audience.

I even miss my little brother. I miss being able to purge into a toilet instead of a sock. I miss having a life, however miserable that life might be.

Life at Golden Slopes is like being in some kind of alternate universe. It's hard to imagine how I'll ever find my way back to reality from here.

"Where the hell is she?" Missy grumbles.

We're all in the dayroom, waiting for Dr. Pardy, who is normally punctual practically to the second, to arrive for group.

"What the hell do you care?" Callie snipes. "It's not like you've got any pressing social engagements."

"To hell with you and your social engagements," Missy snaps. "I'm sick of your snide frickin' comments, Callie. Just shut the hell up, okay?"

I immediately start to tense up, listening to the two of them go at it. I try to take a few deep breaths and practice being mindful of where I'm feeling the tension, like Ali taught us in yoga. My teeth are clenching, my shoulders are approaching ear level, my stomach hurts all of a sudden, and I can feel a knot forming at the back of my head.

"Hey, Missy, take it easy, okay? No need to take Callie's head off," says Tom.

"No one asked you, *Tinkerbell*," Missy hisses. "So just butt out."

Tension in the room kicks up a notch with the Tinkerbell comment. I hate fighting; I always have. At home I go bury myself in my room when Mom and Dad start arguing, which is something they were doing a lot of leading up to the Wedding. But right now I hate Missy dissing Tom more.

"C'mon, Missy, lay off the guy," I say. "He's just trying to help."

"If you ask me, *Tinkerbell* is the one who needs the most help around here," Missy says. "For Christ's sake, the guy's freakin' —"

She stops before she's able to give her supremely unqualified diagnosis of Tom, because Dr. Pardy enters the room — finally.

The good doctor is impeccably dressed, as usual, but she doesn't look her normal intimidatingly beautiful self; instead, she looks pale and strangely tense. I swear there must be something in the water today.

What's also strange is that all the Eating Disorder Nurses — Joe, Kay, and Rose — have entered the room with her. Something is definitely up.

"Please accept my apologies for being late to group," Dr. Pardy says. "I was delayed because I just received some rather distressing news."

Distressing as in what? I think. As in *"There's a huge zit developing on the tip of my nose and I've got a date tonight?"* or as in *"I backed out of the driveway and ran over the neighbor's kid, not to mention the family dog?"* I mean, there are different degrees of distressing, and not all of them warrant being late for group and looking like you've seen a ghost.

"You didn't miss much," Callie says. "Just Missy being a complete moron, that's all."

"Yeah, right. Like you weren't being a total bitch yourself."

Dr. Pardy puts up her hand to stop the bickering.

"Missy and Callie, I will happily allow you to discuss your dispute later. Right now I need to tell you something that most of you will most likely find very upsetting."

I felt the blender in my stomach kick up into high gear. What could she possibly be about to tell us? That none of us were ever going to be let out? That our parents had disowned us for our various transgressions and we were condemned to a life of being observed by the Pee and Eating Police? Now *that* would be distressing.

"I can't tell you how much I regret having to tell you this news," says Dr. Pardy. "I just received word that Helen Swinburne died at five thirty this morning."

Who the hell is Helen Swinburne? I think, until suddenly it strikes me.

"What . . . you mean . . . the Helen who was *here*? Helen the Starver?"

"Yes, Janie. I'm afraid I do mean that Helen."

"No way! I can't believe it. . . . She can't be dead!" Bethany cries. She breaks into hysterical sobbing.

I share Bethany's disbelief that Helen, the Queen of Lean, the Starver-in-Chief, is dead. But my eyes remain dry. I'm numb. I see Helen alone at the table at the end of every meal, sitting in front of a tray of untouched food. I remember the way her thin legs were in constant movement, trying to work off calories she hadn't even consumed. I see her lying on the floor by the pay phone, her eyes rolled back in her head, her limbs twitching. And now I've got a new image to add to my Helen photo gallery — one of her lying there, finally still. Stilled forever . . . dead.

"Wow. That's fucked up," Missy says, shaking her head in disbelief.

"I'll say," agrees Callie, their earlier dispute clearly forgotten in light of the awful news.

"I'm sure this has come as a shock," Dr. Pardy says.

I look over at the Starver side of the room. Bethany is sobbing loudly. Tinka is staring at the floor blankly. Tracey sits, silent tears streaming down her face. Tom's face is as white as his T-shirt.

Even Royce looks pretty shaken up, and he never even met Helen.

"But how come she died?" Tinka asks. "Couldn't they just like feed her through a tube or something? How could they let her starve to death like that?"

"Tinka, no one 'let' Helen starve to death," Dr. Pardy explains. "We tried to help her to the best of our ability. But long-term anorexia takes a dreadful toll on the body — especially the heart. That's how we lost Helen. Her heart failed."

"It's not her heart that failed," I say, before I can shut myself up. "*We* failed. All of us. Well, not just us. Her family. I heard her talking to her dad on the phone that day when she . . . collapsed. He was going on a business trip instead of coming to see her. She was really upset. She thought he didn't love her."

Callie puts her arm around me, which I find surprising, but in a good way. Under her brittle exterior, Callie's got a good heart. Missy hands me a tissue, because if I were normal, I would be crying and need one. But I am so *not* normal right now. Not normal at all.

"Janie, you are not responsible for Helen's death.

None of you are," says Nurse Rose, looking around the room as if daring any of us to feel guilty. "We all tried to help and support Helen to the best of our ability."

The lady doth protest too much, methinks. The *Hamlet* quote pops into my head, because even though Nurse Rose says none of us are responsible, I get the feeling she feels just as awful about Helen's death as I do.

"But why couldn't they save her?" Bethany wails. "She's so young. It's not fair."

"Don't tell me you got to this age and still think life is *FAIR*," Callie yells. "Jesus, you are so freakin' naïve!"

She might not have said it in the kindest way, considering Bethany is so upset, but I have to hand it to Callie because once again she's said exactly what I'm thinking but wouldn't have dared to say. If there's one thing I've learned in my short and miserable life, it's that there is nothing remotely fair about anything. "Fair" is a stupid lie they teach us in nursery school; we spend the rest of our lives trying to get over the discovery that we've been had.

"I'm sure you are all going to be feeling a mix of emotions over the next few days as you process Helen's death," says Dr. Pardy. "Just remember that the nurses and I are all here to help you."

A mix of emotions. I'm already feeling about a zillion feelings — so many I'm not sure where one begins and the other ends. There's such a mess of stuff inside of me my body can't contain it anymore. I wish I could leave group right now and go find a sock.

"I wish it were me instead of Helen," Tracey says, her voice quivering.

"Why is that, Tracey?" Dr. Pardy asks.

"Because she's so young. She has . . . well, had . . . the rest of her life ahead of her. She could have changed. She could have done things. Good things. Happy things. But now . . ."

She breaks off and reaches for the box of tissues.

"It's true that Helen was young and had the potential to live a normal life, Tracey," Dr. Pardy says. "But you have that potential, too. The only difference between Helen and you is about twenty-five years."

Tracey laughs, but it sounds more like a sob.

"That's a lifetime," she says. "If you think about it, it's almost double Helen's lifetime. And haven't you ever heard about how it's impossible to teach an old dog new tricks?"

"Recovery is possible for every person sitting in this room," Dr. Pardy says with quiet determination. "I believe that or else I wouldn't be doing this job. I hope you all do, too."

Tracey sits quietly, shaking her head, tears rolling down her haggard cheeks. I get the impression she's not convinced.

I wonder if it's because her eating disorder has become so much a part of who she is, she doesn't know who she'd be without it. I mean, I don't want to be bulimic for the rest of my life — who in their right mind would want to stick a finger down their throat and puke after every meal or snack? I guess "in their right mind" is the key phrase there. But seriously: Who would want that for themselves — or anyone else, for that matter?

But who am I if I'm not Janie the bulimic? Bulimia has become so much a part of me that I can't remember what it felt like not to binge and purge. It's been this secret that I have hidden from my parents and my friends (well, except for Nancy) and the rest of the world. It's the way I can let off the pressure of always feeling like I'm not smart enough, I'm not thin enough, not pretty enough, not funny enough, just plain not enough enough.

Damn, I feel like puking so badly it hurts. I move restlessly in my chair. I wonder if they'll let me go to the bathroom without the Pee Patrol, given the shock I've experienced. Hmmm. I'm not willing to take a chance on it.

Then I decide to use one of Helen's strategies; I guess it's like some kind of sick memorial to her.

"Can I go to my room and get my journal?" I ask. "I forgot it and I think I should be writing down some of my feelings about this."

Dr. Pardy gives me this X-ray look. I'm sure she sees right through me and she's going to say no and then I'm going to be stuck sitting here for the rest of group unable to listen or concentrate or do anything except think about how desperately I need to purge.

"Can't you wait until after group, Janie?"

"No, I really need to get it now. I need to write these feelings down."

"How about sharing some of your feelings with the group now and then writing them down later?"

No. No way. No how.

"I can't. It's easier for me to write about my feelings than to share them. *Please?*"

"Okay, Janie. But come straight back to group, please."

I practically sprint out of there and down the hall to the privacy of my room. My head is spinning and my stomach churns with this nameless blob of emotions that I can't wait to get out of my body. I grab a sock, stand near the window, and stick my finger down my throat.

What comes out is bitter and acidic. Images of Helen flash through my brain: Helen twitching on the floor, Helen lying dead in a hospital bed with no one there to comfort her. I wonder if her father made it to her bedside. Was her mother there or did she die all alone? Did her parents really not love her or did she just feel that way?

"*Janie!* What do you think you're doing?"

I'm in mid-heave and I try to swallow the evidence but it's too late. I have to exhale into the sock, sealing my seriously snagged, busted fate.

Nurse Rose walks toward me, pulling on a rubber glove. She stretches out her gloved hand. Eww. She can't seriously want me to hand her a puke-filled sock, can she? But disgustingly enough, she does.

"I'm disappointed in you, Janie," she says.

Chalk up another person who thinks Janie Louise Ryman is a Loser with a capital L.

"Join the crowd."

"I thought you were genuinely committed to your recovery. What happened?"

"I guess recovery is just another thing I'm not good at."

"Well, I want to *help* you be good at it, Janie. All of

us do. But we need your cooperation. We need you to *want* to be healthy."

"Of course I *want* to be healthy. Who doesn't?"

Nurse Rose sits on the bed, still clutching the sock of puke. She looks tired and sad, all of a sudden. I can't believe the smell isn't making her retch.

"Helen didn't, for one." She sighs. "We just couldn't reach her. But you, Janie . . . I know you can do this if you'll allow us to help you."

There's something I don't understand.

"Nurse Rose . . . *why* didn't Helen want to get better? Like I can understand that she wanted to be thinner — we *all* do — but why would she let it go on so long that she *died*? I mean if she really wanted to die, why didn't she just take pills or . . . I don't know . . . slit her wrists or something?"

"Oh, Janie, I wish I knew." Nurse Rose looks so defeated. "But I don't think Helen *wanted* to die. Patients like Helen seem to have this almost . . . *magical idea* that they can do with their bodies as they please. It's almost like they reject the possibility that they'll die because they're so focused on staying in control of how few calories they can put in their body each day."

"But she must have known that if she didn't eat, she might die. How could she not?"

Nurse Rose looks me in the eye. "Janie, you know that bulimia can be fatal, don't you?"

"Well . . . yeah. But that's only people with *serious* bulimia. You know, who've had it for a long time."

She shakes her head and gives me a stern glance.

"That's not necessarily true. But my point is that you know that by continuing to binge and purge, you risk ending up in a coma or dying. But you still do it. In fact, you're so intent on continuing to do it, you're willing to lie to Dr. Pardy and sneak into your room to throw up into a *sock*."

My face feels hot as I stare down at the stained linoleum. When you put it that way, it sounds . . . pretty bad.

"What I'm trying to tell you is that there's knowing and there's *knowing*. You know that bingeing and purging is bad for you, but you don't *know* it, because if you did, you wouldn't continue to do it. Maybe you think that the danger doesn't apply to *you*? Because if that's the case, I'm here to tell you that it *does*."

I keep my gaze focused on the floor.

"No. . . . I don't think it's because of that. It's more like . . . well, when I started, you know, purging, I was in control of it, like I could choose to be bulimic when I wanted to be," I tell her. "But after a while, I guess . . . well, now I feel like the bulimia is in control of me instead. And I can't stop it. I just can't."

Nurse Rose pats me on the knee.

"You *can* stop it, Janie. And I'm here to help you. So is Dr. Pardy. All of us here at Golden Slopes really *want* to help you — but you have to want to help yourself."

She stands up.

"I'm going to have to report this, you know."

"Why? Can't you just give me a break?" I plead. "I mean, this was an extreme circumstance with Helen dying and all. If you tell Dr. Pardy she's going to make me stay in here longer, and I want to go home. *Please?*"

"Janie, you're always going to face challenging situations in life, and part of recovery is learning to find more constructive — and less self-destructive — ways of dealing with them. I'm sorry, but the rules are the rules, and you broke one. A big one. You'll have to face the consequences."

Whatever warm fuzzies I was feeling toward Nurse Rose for being so understanding and encouraging evaporate instantly. I should have remembered that underneath her kind and caring exterior, she's an enemy agent.

"Come on, grab your journal and let's get you back to group before it's over. Dr. Pardy must be wondering what happened to you."

I feel awful as Nurse Rose shepherds me back to the dayroom. Is she going to rat me out to Dr. Pardy in front of the whole group? And what are the "consequences" going to be? More jail time? Going to bed without dinner? (Bet the Starvers would love that.)

Dr. Pardy doesn't say anything when I rejoin the group, and thankfully neither does Nurse Rose. But I find it hard to focus on what's going on for the rest of the session because I'm too busy worrying about what Dr. Pardy is going to say when she finds out, and what kind of gruesome punishment awaits me.

CHAPTER 10

July 29th

I HATE THIS PLACE!!! I HATE THIS PLACE!!!! I HATE THIS FUCKING PLACE!!!!! It's NOT helping me — if anything IT'S MAKING ME CRAZIER!!! I HATE THIS GODDAMN MISERABLE SHITHOLE!!!

July 30th

Yesterday was a Grade A Suckfest. It started off in my private session with Dr. Pardy. She read me the Riot Act for my sock-puking transgression. Apparently the landscapers had brought to her attention that they'd been finding vomity socks on the lawn, but she hadn't been sure from whose room they'd originated until Nurse Rose snagged me in pukus interruptus. *I got the* blah blah blah *"disappointed in you"* blah blah blah *"want to help you"* blah diddy blah blah *"need to be committed to recovery"* blah blah blah *speech.*

Then Dr. Pardy got out her rod and started trying to fish my brain: "What emotion were you feeling the moment before you picked up the sock?" *blah blah blah and* "Can you think of something you could do to distract yourself when you feel like purging?" *blah diddy blah blah blah.*

The thing is, I wasn't lying when I answered "I don't know" to both questions. Even if I did know, I wouldn't want to tell her, but I really don't know. So I'm under orders to try to sit with my emotions when I feel the urge to purge, and report back to her with what it is, exactly, that I'm feeling. Or, as Dr. Pardy put it, that I would rather purge than allow myself to feel.

Then, after the lecturing and fishing and prodding came the punishment. No phone privileges for five days (Five days!!! They expect me to still be stuck here after five freakin' days?!!!!!) and, worst of all, no visitors other than my immediate family. And that's what totally, utterly, and completely sucks, because Kelsey was going to visit me this afternoon. She promised to bring me some good books and some up-to-date gossip magazines. All Mom and Dad bring me are an endless stream of self-help books like How Thinking Positive Can Change Your Life *(Dad's choice) and* Eating Disorders: A Plan for Recovery *(Mom's).*

When I got out of there, I wanted to purge so badly, but I couldn't because they've got people watching me all the time. So I was sitting there, desperate because I couldn't purge and feeling like

I was going to explode with some feeling that I couldn't name but I hated to have inside me. Then it struck me — I was angry. I was so fucking pissed off I wanted to hit someone or something. Because I couldn't see Kelsey and I can't even talk to her on the phone. Because I'm going to be stuck in this hellhole for at least another five days, if not longer, and because these people just don't understand me. Because I hate Dr. Pardy who probably doesn't have to worry about anything because she's thin and gorgeous and has great clothes and I'll bet she has a boyfriend or a husband who is as gorgeous as Matt Lewis, but who actually cares about her.

To make matters worse, they changed my room so I have a roommate, and it's Callie of all people. Originally they were going to put a new Starver girl called Eileen, who just arrived today, into my room, which wouldn't have been so bad but Callie — argh! She's been lashing out at everyone over the slightest thing, and ragging on everyone in group — especially Tom for some reason. It's like she's really got it in for him. I don't understand why — if anyone, I'd think she'd have it in for Royce because he's more like your typical Male Chauvinist Pig — but no, she's picking on Tom. It really pisses me off.

It's strange because now that I've figured out what the feeling is, I find that I'm walking around with my teeth clenched and my shoulders tense like I can't stop being mad. Maybe I'll see if I can get one of the nurses to take a group of us to the gym tonight. They only let the Barfers go, because the Starvers aren't allowed to exercise, but they keep a pretty strict eye on us Barfers, too, in case we turn into "exercise bulimics" — people who purge by exercising off every single calorie they eat instead of by barfing. That is so totally not me. I guess I'm a "lazy bulimic" — I'd much rather take the easy way out and stick my finger down my throat than have to exercise constantly. But right now I feel like I could do with sweating it out a little. After all, I'm under doctor's orders to find some "alternative strategies," aren't I? And after the family therapy session with my parents and Dr. Pardy that's sched-uled for this morning, I bet I'm going to need some kind of stress relief.

Mom and Dad are sitting stiff as two mannequins when I walk into Dr. Pardy's office. You know how you can sense that people have been discussing you? Except I bet they've been *dissecting* me — trying to figure out what is wrong so they can "fix" me, turning me back into the ideal daughter who doesn't have problems, or if she *does* have problems keeps them well hidden so her parents don't have to deal with them.

Dr. Pardy has put on her geek-chic glasses — I won-der if it's to give her authority with an alpha male like Dad. Mom looks like she's been crying again. Argh.

"Come in and take a seat, Janie," Dr. Pardy says. "Make yourself comfortable."

Make yourself comfortable? Puh-leeze! Who on earth would feel comfortable when they have three adults sitting there waiting to tell them that they're totally screwed up?

I take a seat on the sofa, as far away from my parents as I can, kick off my sneakers (pretty easy when they've removed your laces so you don't hang yourself), and hug my knees to my chest. I'm sure Dr. P is noting my "defensive body language" in her chart, but I don't care.

"We're here to discuss what changes could be made at home in order to support your recovery when you leave Golden Slopes," Dr. Pardy says. "I've been getting your parents' views on the subject, but we'd like to hear what you have to say, too."

Oh, no. I'm not falling into *that* trap.

"Um . . . I dunno. I can't really think of anything."

"Janie, your parents were telling me how this came as a shock to them, because you're an honor student and such a talented actress. Obviously, you're very good at masking your problems."

Obviously.

"Well, they said I was a good actress, didn't they?"

"Enough lip, Janie," Dad says. His voice is almost as tight and stiff as his posture. He hates shrinks almost as much as he hates divorce lawyers.

Dr. Pardy holds up a hand to Dad to shush him. She clearly doesn't realize that she's taking her life in her hands.

"That's true. They did. However, I think your parents were referring to your skills onstage, rather than at home."

"Yeah, well. They always call me a drama queen at home, too, so why should things be any different?"

"*Are* you a 'drama queen' at home?"

Dad opens his mouth to speak but gets the shushing hand again from Dr. Pardy. Amazingly, he *does* shush.

"Well, obviously I am — I mean, otherwise I wouldn't be in here, would I?"

"Janie, I think you're in here for more reasons than being a 'drama queen,' don't you?" she says.

"I guess."

"Getting drunk and throwing up at your sister's wedding, shaming yourself and your entire family would top *my* list," Dad says.

"Hal, please . . ."

Dad cuts Mom off before she can tell him to not make a scene.

"It's no use pussyfooting around this, Carole," he says. "Maybe that's part of the problem with Janie — that you've indulged her."

"*I've* indulged her?" Mom says, her voice still watery, yet now with an unmistakable edge. "So this is all *my* fault, is it?"

"You've got to admit that you spoil her rotten," Dad replies, seemingly oblivious to Mom's rising irritation. "At least Clarissa brought up Jenny with a firm hand."

Oh, boy. Now he's done it. He's used the C-word on Mom. It's like instant nuclear fission.

"If Clarissa was so *perfect*, Hal, then why didn't you stay married to *her*, for crying out loud?" Mom says, her voice rising in intensity with each word that manages to squeeze its way out from between her gritted teeth. "I mean you obviously consider her the perfect mother, who was able to provide you with a perfect daughter...something that I have clearly failed to do."

I want to disappear into the floor. I hate that Dr. Pardy is seeing my parents fight like this. I hate that my parents are fighting, period. But most of all, I hate the fact that my parents think I'm the ultimate in imperfect daughters, that my screwedupness makes my mother feel like a failure. It's my fault that they are fighting at all. I bet they'd be happier if I were dead. I want to purge, to empty myself, so that I can feel light and pure again, but I can't because there's no way Dr. Pardy is going to let me out of here without someone watching my every move.

Instead, I pick something to stare at — a picture on Dr. Pardy's wall of a woman and a little girl walking in a field of red poppies. It's a print of some famous painting, I think by Monet or one of those other Impressionist guys. I try to take myself away from this room, from these feelings — from this miserable life of mine. I take myself to that field, under the azure sky and white cottony clouds that float overhead, imagining myself as the girl in the picture, walking beside her mother through the sea of red flowers. I bet you anything that the mother in that picture didn't think her daughter was a complete loser who would end up in a psych ward and make her feel like a failure as a parent. I want to be that girl, even if she is just pigment on canvas. I want to be her more than anything *because she doesn't have to feel*.

I still hear the sounds of my parents' raised voices, but it's like being underwater and having someone talk to you from the surface; you know they're saying words but all you hear are diluted waves of sound. I started doing this at the dinner table when my parents started fighting about the Wedding; I take myself to a secret place inside where I don't have to listen to the angry words. The thing is, it's getting harder and harder to come back.

"Janie . . . are you with us?"

Dr. Pardy's voice ripples through the water over the distant hum of my parents' anger.

Reluctantly, I pull myself away from the field of poppies and back into the grim reality of the anger-filled room.

"What?"

"Janie, I think it would be best if I spoke to your parents in private for a while. Why don't you wait for us in the dayroom?"

She doesn't have to tell me twice. I practically leap out of the chair, I'm so anxious to get the hell out of there.

"Sure — see ya."

I look back as I exit the room to see my parents are sitting there stony-faced. My father's arms are crossed across his chest and his body is turned away from my mother. Mom is crying again, *surprise, surprise*. It's so unfair; she's crying up a freakin' river and I can't even shed a tear.

Tom and Tinka are in the dayroom playing Scrabble when I get there. Tinka's really good at Scrabble — she's incredibly smart. When she's not busy starving, she's a sophomore at Harvard.

"Hey, how was the grand meeting *en famille*?" Tom asks.

I look at his letter tray and the board and figure I can do him a gaming favor and answer at the same time.

"S-U-C-K-E-D," I spell out. "And that's a triple word score for you!"

"That's awesome," he says. "Well, about the triple word score. Sorry that the meeting sucked."

"Yeah, awesome is certainly not a word my parents would use in the same sentence as yours truly right about now."

"I hate when we have those family therapy meetings," Tinka says. "I get the impression that my parents liked it better when they didn't have to deal with me. Like, it's easier for them to have me being superachieving and anorexic than it is for them to have to face that their expectations for me might have something to do with the fact that I'm so screwed up."

"Ditto," I say. "Well, except for the anorexia part. I'm sure my parents liked it better when I just did my homework, went to play practice, got good grades, and puked my dinner up quietly in the bathroom. I bet I could have gone on being bulimic for years if I hadn't made such a scene at Jenny's wedding."

"Yeah, well, that's the difference between being bulimic and anorexic," Tom says. "Being anorexic is a lot harder to hide. Unless you're trying to hide it from my dad, that is. But in his case I think it's more that he didn't *want* to see than that he *didn't* see."

"Funny you should mention that," Tinka says, grinning. She lays down D-E-N-I-A-L. "And that's got a triple letter score!"

"And here they keep trying to tell us that denial is bad for us," I tell her. "Obviously not in *every* situation."

"Frankly, I think a little denial is healthy," Tom says. "It's about the only thing that keeps me sane."

Tinka and I look at each other and burst out laughing.

"Sane being a relative term in a place like this," she says.

Tom joins in the laughter — but mine fades when I see Dr. Pardy standing in the doorway.

"Janie, please come join us again," she says.

I give Tom and Tinka a *help me!* glance.

"Good luck," Tom whispers. "Don't let the bastards . . . uh . . . I mean *them* . . . get you down."

"Not easy," I whisper back. "Not easy at all."

Mom's eyes are even redder than before, but at least my parents are holding hands, so Dr. Pardy must have helped them work out Dad's dropping of the C-bomb. I wonder if she'd be as good at working out *my* problems if I actually volunteered to let her into my head. I'm not willing to take the risk, because I'm worried that if she finds out just how completely screwed up I am, she'll *never* let me out of this place.

"I've been speaking to your parents about how family conflict can feed into eating disorders. But I wanted to give you an opportunity to voice any thoughts about how your parents — and the rest of your family — might be able to give you additional support."

How can my family support me? Let me count the ways. . . . There are so many I can think of — but instead I say, "I dunno."

"Well, perhaps I'll kick things off by sharing a few things I've discussed with your parents," says Dr. Pardy. "Firstly, as part of your release plan from Golden Slopes, we require that you see a therapist weekly. I've also recommended that you attend an outpatient eating disorders group."

"But — how will I ever be able to go to play practice if I have all these shrink appointments?" I protest.

"Play practice isn't so important," Dad pronounces. "Getting better is."

I feel something swelling inside me — something huge and terrifying. I feel like if I don't let it out, I'll explode, but if I do let it out . . . I don't know, it's just too frightening to contemplate. So I just sit there, fixing my eyes on the picture of the poppy field, every breath hurting because of the effort it takes to keep this insidious growth inside me.

"How do you feel about what you father said, Janie?" Dr. Pardy asks. She's trying to fish again. She wants to stick that hook inside me and drag this thing out, but I'm so not going to let her. I swear I'm not.

"He's right, of course," I say in a monotone. "Getting better is important."

There. I've said what you all want to hear. Now let me the fuck out of this place, okay?

"We want Janie to be able to come home," Mom sniffs, dabbing her eyes again. "I hate to see you in this place," she adds, fixing me with her tearful gaze.

Well, I sure as hell don't miss hearing you and Dad fight, or seeing you crying all the frickin' time when I'm the one locked up in here and you're not.

"When might Janie be released?" Dad asks.

I bet he's sick of paying the $500-a-day co-pay. But I'm glad he asked the question, because I want to know the answer to that myself.

"It's too early to be talking about a discharge date," Dr. Pardy says. I feel that growth inside me swell even more when I hear that. It's so big I can barely breathe or swallow.

"Janie has been making progress," Dr. Pardy continues. "But we had a bit of a setback recently and I need to be convinced that she's truly committed to her recovery before I can even begin to *think* about releasing her from the hospital."

"Setback? What setback?" Mom sniffs. Oh, jeez — don't let her start crying again.

"Of course she's committed to her recovery — aren't you, Pussycat?" Dad says.

I thought I told him never to call me that in public. If I have to stay in this room another minute, I'll die. Or at least that's how it feels. I really don't want to be in here when Dr. Pardy tells my parents about my sock-puking transgression.

"Can I go now — *please*?" I beg Dr. Pardy. "I think Joe is taking a bunch of us to the gym and I *really* need to go."

"That's fine, Janie. I'll finish up with your parents."

"Bye, Mom. Bye, Dad. See you soon."

"Bye, sweetie," Dad says. "Hang in there. Keep your chin up. Think positive."

Any more clichés you'd like to add before I leave?

Mom presses my head to her silk-clad shoulder.

"Take care of yourself, darling. We miss you at home."

I disentangle myself from her soggy embrace.

"Yeah, miss you, too. See ya."

And then I'm free. Or at least free from that room — and for now, that feels good enough.

I walk over to the nurses' station.

"Joe, can you take us over to the gym soon? I *really* need to go."

"Sure," Joe says. "We can leave in about five minutes." He eyes me quizzically. "Had a rough family meeting, did you?"

You are so *not going to trap me, Joe.*

"No, it was really helpful," I lie, feeling that growth in my chest again, "Yeah, superhelpful."

He doesn't look convinced, but tells me he'll call me when he's ready to take me. I head to my room to change into shorts and a T-shirt.

Callie is sprawled across her bed, reading.

"Hey, what's that?"

She snaps the book shut and shoves it behind her back.

"Nothing," she says.

"C'mon, tell me," I say, pulling a pair of shorts out of the drawer.

"None of your business," Callie says. "Who elected you to the Book Police?"

Well, excuse me for breathing.

"What the hell is your problem, Callie? I just like to talk about books, okay?"

"Yeah, well I *don't*. I prefer *reading* them."

I pull on my shorts.

"Fine, be that way. I'll leave you to read in peace. I'm going to the gym."

As I leave the room, I can't help wondering yet again what the hell is eating Callie. But frankly, I'm more worried about what the hell is eating *me*. I still feel the I.G. (Insidious Growth) inside me, and it's like I'm choking for air. I just hope a few flights of StairMaster help me work the damn thing out.

Royce and Missy join the gym excursion, as well as a couple of the generally psycho people. The General Psychos and Royce head to the basketball court for some two-on-two. Missy gets on the treadmill. It looks like she lost a few pounds since she's been in here, not that we're supposed to care about stuff like that. But seriously, who wouldn't?

I'm about to go on the elliptical when Joe calls me over and hands me a pair of boxing gloves.

"What am I supposed to do with *these*?" I ask, holding them at arm's length.

"Well, putting them on your *hands* would be a good start," he says.

I never figured Nurse Joe for a sense of humor.

"But why would I want to do *that*?"

"Because if you hit this here punching bag without them, you'll seriously hurt your knuckles, that's why."

I start to say that I don't want to hit the punching bag, that I, Janie Louise Ryman, was not brought up to punch things, but then I think of Dad saying that play practice doesn't matter and I pull the gloves on.

Joe laughs at my first attempt at a punch.

"C'mon, Janie! You can do better than that. You punch like a girl!"

I glare at him.

"This might have escaped your notice, Joe, but I AM a girl."

"True. But it doesn't mean you have to punch like one. Here, let me show you."

He pulls on a pair of gloves and starts whaling on the bag like it's a mugger who tried to steal his wallet.

"I can't do that!" I protest.

"Sure you can," he tells me. "Just throw from the shoulder, not from the elbow."

He shows me again.

The first few times I feel stupid. But Joe corrects my form and encourages me to try again.

I do. Again and again. I punch that bag, harder and harder, faster and faster. "Play practice isn't important *my ass*!" I mutter, as I smash my fists into the bag, over and over again.

It feels *so* good. The Insidious Growth shrinks a little with each blow. After ten minutes I've got sweat dripping from my face and trickling between my breasts but I can't stop.

"Feels good, doesn't it?" Joe says. "I always work out on the bag when I'm mad."

"I'm not mad," I say automatically.

He just looks at me.

"Really, I'm not. I just . . . oh, okay, I'll admit it. I'm *fucking furious*."

Joe grins from ear to ear. "I thought that might be the case when I saw you after your family meeting."

"But . . . how did you know? I didn't even know it myself right then."

"Janie, I was a sergeant in the Marines. You don't

spend that much time with a bunch of hotheaded nineteen-year-olds without being able to recognize someone who is seriously pissed off but bottling it all up inside."

So I was right about GI Joe.

"I didn't know that what I was feeling was mad. It just felt like . . . like this cancerous growth inside that was strangling me."

"That's what anger does if you don't let it out," Joe says, suddenly serious. "Believe me, I know. I was one hell of an angry kid. I'm not exaggerating when I say the Marines saved my life."

He sits on the bench and gestures for me to sit, too.

"I'm not saying that you should start to pick fights or break things when you're angry," Joe says. "But you'll be a lot happier — and healthier, too — if you can find a way to let the mad out in a constructive way. Have you ever tried kickboxing?"

"No. I've never even thought about it. But actually now that I've figured out how much fun it is to punch things, I'll give it a try. It'll help me when I star in *Charlie's Angels Six*."

Amazingly, Joe laughs. I didn't think the guy *ever* laughed.

"You sure as hell better invite me to the premiere when you do," he says. "I've always dreamed about going to one of those fancy schmancy Hollywood parties."

"It's a deal," I tell him. "And . . . Joe . . . thanks."

CHAPTER ELEVEN

August 1st

I got Joe to take me back to the gym yesterday, and I had another session on the punching bag. It's like now that I realized that I'm mad, I just want to punch the shit out of the thing morning, noon, and night. I pretend it's Matt Lewis, I pretend it's my dad and then my mom. I even pretend it's Dr. Pardy. I wonder if I'd have started sticking my finger down my throat if I'd known how good it felt to punch things.

The first time I purged was about two years ago, I think. Mom took Harry and me out for Chinese, because Dad was traveling. I was starving when we got to the restaurant because I'd had late play practice and hadn't had much for lunch, so as soon as they put the crispy noodles and duck sauce on the table I practically inhaled the entire bowl, much to Harry's chagrin because those are one of the few things he likes at the Chinese restaurant. I wolfed down a pretty good sizeable portion of cold sesame noodles, too, and then, even though I was starting to feel kind of full, I couldn't not eat the main course or else I'd get a lecture from Mom about filling up on the crispy noodles — even though she doesn't seem to care if Harry does that.

By the time the waiter brought the bill along with the fortune cookies and orange slices, my stomach felt stuffed and huge, like I'd swallowed an oversize watermelon. I felt awful on the way home in the car — it was painful being that full.

When we got home, I went up to my room to do my homework, but it was impossible to concentrate.

You know how when you've got a stomach bug and you feel really awful and then you finally throw up and you feel better? I figured that if I threw up a little bit, maybe it would relieve some of the painful pressure in my stomach. So I went into my bath-room — that's one advantage of having a father who's loaded, having your own bathroom — and stuck my finger down my throat. That time I didn't completely purge. I did just what I set out to do, which was relieve some of the full feeling, and I was right — it did feel better afterward.

So in the beginning it was only once in a while — I hadn't started bingeing then. Purging was just a way to relieve the full when I'd eaten a lit-tle bit too much. I was in control of it — or so I thought.

I can't tell you exactly when it *started controlling* me, *but things started going downhill in a hurry at the beginning of last summer.*

What happened? It's hard to say it was any one thing. Jenny and Brad announced their engagement, triggering endless discussions about the Wedding. Then the fights started, in a seemingly endless series of permutations — Dad vs. Clarissa, Clarissa vs. Mom, Mom vs. Dad, Jenny vs. Dad. I couldn't stand it. You never knew how it was going to be at home — or who was going to be mad at whom.

I don't know if it was because of the fighting that I started bingeing. That was definitely a factor. But there were other things. Kelsey was away most of the summer, working as a junior counselor at a sleepaway camp for vegetarians. Danny was dating Nicole Hartman and they were spending every waking moment together when he wasn't at work, so he didn't have much time for me. I had other friends — it's not like I was a complete loser — but without Kelsey and Danny around I felt kind of lonely, not to mention bored. I couldn't get a good summer job because my parents were taking us to Europe for three weeks, so I ended up working at the local ice cream parlor. When things were slow and I was really bored and depressed, I'd make myself these elaborate sundaes with hot fudge sauce, whipped cream, and jimmies and then go make myself throw up in the employee restroom.

Once school started, it got worse, because it was much more intense than sophomore year, what with having to worry about taking the SATs and the pressure of taking two AP classes on top of the usual honors stuff. By the time I got the lead in Anne Frank, *which was a dream come true but even more pressure, I was bingeing and purging at least three times a day, sometimes more.*

So there you have it — my sorry tale. That's how something I thought I controlled ended up controlling me.

When Callie leaves the room to take a shower in the morning, I sneak a look under her pillow and find the book that she's been so secretive about reading. The title freaks me out — *Incest: A Guide for Survivors.* Does this mean that Callie . . . could it possibly be that she . . . I can't even bear to think about it, or who it might be that did it . . . like what if it's her father? Or her brother? Does she even have a brother? I can't remember.

I slide the book back under her pillow and lie down on my bed, my head spinning as I try to take it in. I guess it would explain a lot about Callie — the cutting, her comment that being bitchy is "the only way to get by." But the thought of it . . . it's too horrible for words.

No wonder she's got so many scars. But the scars on the outside can't be anything compared to the scars she's got on the inside . . . if that's what she's been through.

Part of me wants to stay in the room and talk to her about it, to show her that I care, to tell her that I'll try to understand if she's being bitchy — that it's just because of what she has to deal with. But another part of me is scared — scared she'll be mad at me for invading her privacy, scared to be drawn into that much pain when I feel so much of my own.

I'm ashamed to say the scared part wins. I make sure I leave the room before she gets back so I don't have to see her till breakfast, when there'll be plenty of other people around. Chalk up another thing that I suck at — being a good friend.

The one good thing about breakfast is that most of what I have is supposed to be cold, so it doesn't matter if the Starvers are late to the table. The first morning after I get out of here, I'm going to the diner for pancakes, waffles, and maybe even blintzes. Okay, maybe not all at once. But I'm looking forward to having a cooked breakfast where everything is warm again.

Tom is sitting across the table from me, next to Royce, who is inhaling a bowl of Total while talking to Missy. Tom, being a Starver, has a big breakfast to get down: eggs, toast, and cereal.

"Royce, could you pass the salt and pepper, please?" Tom says.

Royce either doesn't hear or is purposely ignoring him. I hope it's not the latter.

"Uh ... Royce — do you mind passing the salt and pepper?" Tom repeats, a little louder this time.

Missy giggles. She's been flirting with Royce like crazy, even though (*a*) you're not allowed to have relationships and (*b*) Royce supposedly has a girlfriend, even if he is still pissed at her for ratting him out to the wrestling coach and landing him in here. I can't believe Royce is falling for it, but he's pretty busy flirting back. Too busy flirting to pass Tom the condiments, obviously.

I roll my eyes at Tom and he shrugs his slender shoulders. Finally, he just reaches across Royce and grasps the S&P shakers.

"What the hell are you doing, you *faggot*! *Get the hell off of me!*"

I can't believe what I just heard.

"Jesus, Royce, I was just getting the salt and pepper since you were too *busy* to pass it to me."

"Why the hell didn't you *ask* me for it, then, instead of touching me like that?"

"He did ask you, *moron*! *Twice*," I tell Royce. "You were just too busy flirting with Missy to hear."

"Don't listen to her," Missy says. "She's just jealous."

"*Jealous?!* What drugs did they put *you* on today?"

Royce is still hassling Tom.

"Why don't you just stand up and admit that you're a faggot, instead of trying to touch me on the sly?"

"Why don't you just shut up, *idiot*!" I shout. "*Leave Tom alone!*"

I look over at Tom, who is pale and shaking. Suddenly I see a strange, determined look cross his face and he pushes back his chair and stands up.

"Yeah. Okay. News flash! I'm gay. A faggot, as Mr. Neanderthal here cares to describe me. You've heard it here first, because my homophobic friend just helped me to say it out loud."

"Well, DUH!" Missy says.

Wow. I mean, I had my suspicions. But I'll admit I

never thought Tom was going to come out and say it. I want to cheer.

Tom looks down at Royce, who is sitting there with his mouth hanging open.

"There. Are you satisfied, asshole?"

Callie stands up and starts clapping.

"Bravo, Tommy-boy. About time you came out."

I join her in the ovation. Eventually the entire table (well, except for Royce, who is looking decidedly uncomfortable) is standing and clapping. Tom's flushed face shows a strange mixture of elation and *what the hell have I done?* Nurse Kay looks on, smiling. (Where the hell was she when Royce was calling Tom a faggot?) I bet this is going to be written up in Tom's notes. But what the hell, it can only be a good thing for him to admit to himself that he's gay, right?

Tom sits next to me in art therapy. He's alternating between ecstatic and petrified.

"It's such a relief to have it out in the open...to finally be able to admit this to people. I feel like I'm going to float away from the lightness of it."

"Well, watch out if you do that, because no doubt Royce will call you a fairy."

Tom gives me a look. We both crack up.

I'm busy making a figurine out of clay. The assignment is to make an image of ourselves as we would like to be. Right now I'm looking decidedly like an alien, which might be how I feel now, but sure as hell isn't the way I want to be in the future.

"You know, I bet it was hard work denying that there was any remote possibility of you being gay."

Tom laughs. "Oh, yeah. I'm sure that's part of the lightness — not having to spend all that energy on pretending I'm not feeling what I'm feeling."

He's serious, suddenly.

"But how the hell am I going to tell *my parents*? My father is going to beat the crap out of me. Then he'll tell me he knew it all along and give the whole spiel about how he can't believe a wimp like me came out of his loins."

"He *never* said that to you!"

"Wanna make a bet?"

After having seen Tom's dad in action, and especially after Tom's depiction of him in psychodrama, I'm not sure that's a bet I want to take.

"Well, you know that Nurse Kay has reported your change of sexual orientation to Dr. Pardy by now, seeing as the Walls Have Ears in this place. Why don't you ask *her* about how to cope with telling your parents?"

"Yeah . . . and then maybe I can act it out in psychodrama for practice."

"Now *that's* a session I wouldn't want to miss," I joke.

"Believe me, I wish I *could* miss it. I'm just freaked about how it's going to go down with my parents. Well, my dad really, because I don't think my mom will care either way. But my dad . . . I just know my dad will blame the fact that I'm queer on my mother."

"Look, Tom, if your parents' marriage falls apart just because you admit you're gay, it can't have been in all that great shape to begin with, can it?"

"Well . . . no . . . I guess not."

"I mean, for Pete's sake, your dad is *cheating on your mother* — if you want to blame anyone for their marriage falling apart, you should blame him, not yourself, right?"

Tom doesn't answer me right away. He's busy trying to reform the clay version of himself. I notice that he's making himself bigger than he was the first time.

"Yeah . . . I guess you're right." He looks at me and smiles. "How'd you get to be so smart, anyway?"

I almost fall off my stool.

"*ME?!* Smart? Yeah, right! You're talking to Ms. Sock Puker here, remember?"

Tom covers my clay-covered hand with his.

"Don't underestimate yourself, Janie. It's something you do a lot. I've noticed that about you."

I get seriously embarrassed, like I do whenever someone compliments me. I think it's because I feel like if they really knew me, they wouldn't be saying nice stuff.

"Anyway, we'd better finish these," I say, trying to change the subject. "I don't want the art therapy teacher to think that I really *want* to look like some space creature."

Tom gives me a look to let me know that he *knows* I'm trying to change the subject.

"Yeah, and I sure as hell don't want her to think that I want to look like Frankenstein's aborted love child, do I?"

Tom talks to Dr. Pardy after lunch, and when we meet up at the dinner table later that evening, he's looking a bit more relaxed.

"She said she'd help me with telling my parents — that we can do it in one of our family meetings," he says. "She said that even though this has to be a difficult thing to do, it's important for me to live an authentic life."

An authentic life. I wonder how exactly you go about living one. I wonder what kind of person I would be if I were able to do it.

"Anyway, Dr. Pardy said that I shouldn't let my anxiety about the state of my parents' marriage stop me from telling them that I'm gay, because although that affects me, what goes on in their marriage is really between the two of them. It's not something that I have any control over."

Wow. Dr. Pardy is actually making sense where Tom is concerned. I wonder why she doesn't seem to do a whole lot for me. I wonder if it's because she just thinks I'm this hopeless case and it's not worth making the effort. Now *there's* a depressing thought.

When Royce arrives for dinner, he goes to sit at the opposite end of the table, as far away from Tom and me as possible. But Tom gets up and walks over to him.

"I'd like to shake your hand and thank you for helping me to come out of the closet, but you'd probably think I'm making a pass at you, so I'll just salute instead."

And he does. I'm pleased to see Royce looks sheepish.

"Yeah, whatever," Royce mutters, but apparently he's still unable to look Tom in the eye.

Well, baby steps, I guess.

Nurse Kay arrives and starts distributing trays. I rip off the foil from my dinner. It's chicken in a mushroomy type sauce, broccoli, and salad, with Jell-O for dessert. At least Starvers roundup went quickly tonight, so the chicken is still hot. I think this is the first really hot meal I've eaten since I came here and had to deal with that stupid rule that says we have to wait for everyone to be at the table before we can eat. It's bad enough that we eating disorder patients have to eat separately from the other, generally screwed-up people, but I really think they should have separate tables for the Starvers and the Barfers, since we *want* to eat and they don't. That way the Barfers would always get hot food instead of everything being lukewarm because some stupid Starver was off playing hide-and-seek with the nurses. Although then I wouldn't be able to eat at the same table as Tom, and I like talking to him at meals. I like talking to him at any time, really. I almost wish he weren't gay and that I were attracted to him. Maybe that's something I need to explore in my therapy — why it's so much easier to talk to Tom, who as it happens is gay, than to guys like Matt Lewis, who I was wildly attracted to — even if he's an asshole. Or maybe it's *because* he's an asshole. Definitely to be explored.

I finish the chicken and move on to the salad. Tom has eaten about four bites of chicken and is sitting there staring despondently at his tray.

"Eat up, Tommy-boy. You want out of this place, right?" I say.

"Yeah. But if I eat all this I think *I'll* want to puke. And you know that's not usually my style," he says in an undertone, so the Food Police don't hear.

I look at him, curious.

"Have you ever made yourself puke?" I whisper.

"Once in a while. Sometimes after soccer practice I get so hungry that I eat a *lot* of calories. More than I want to. So I have, on occasion, gone into the bathroom to make myself puke. I mean, if it works for my mother, why shouldn't it work for me?"

Why indeed. No wonder Tom feels comfortable hanging with the Barfers. He's a closet Barfer himself.

I'm busy thinking about Tom and his closet puking when all of a sudden I spot something awful on my tray. No, not a bug or a worm — it's not that kind of awful. Something that's just awful to *me* because I hate eating it — a slice of cucumber.

I've hated cucumber for as long as I can remember. My mom can't understand it: *"They don't even taste like anything. How can you hate them so much?"*

The answer is I don't *know* why I hate them so much. I just do. It's like asking why Harry hates eating food with any nutritional value.

"Oh, damn," I say. "There's cucumber in this."

"So?" Tom says.

"I hate cucumbers."

"How can you hate cucumber? It doesn't even have a taste."

Here we go again . . .

"It *does* have a taste," I argue. "It tastes like . . . cucumber."

"Well you're stuck eating it unless you want to go the Ensure route," he says.

"We'll see."

I raise my hand so Nurse Kay will come over.

"What's up, Janie?" Nurse Kay asks.

"There's cucumber in my salad, and I hate cucumber."

She doesn't give me the "it doesn't have a taste" bull, but her answer is even worse.

"I'm afraid you'll have to eat it anyway, Janie. Either that or I can get you a can of Ensure."

"But I've already eaten most of my meal, and I'll be happy to eat something else instead — like I'll eat double the amount of tomato if you'll exchange it for the cucumber."

"We can swap," Tom offers. "Janie can have my tomato, and I'll eat her cucumber."

I flash him a grateful smile, but Nurse Kay's having none of it.

"It's kind of you to offer, Tom, but Janie has to eat all of her own dinner. You're not allowed to exchange meals."

"We're not exchanging *meals*, we're just exchanging *salad vegetables*," I protest. "And it's not like I'm trying to get out of eating or anything. I'll have *five times* the amount of tomato as long as I don't have to eat the cucumber."

"I hear what you're saying, Janie, but the rules are clear," Nurse Kay says.

I take it back. She's not one of the good guys after all. She's just as much of a Food Nazi as Nurse Rose and Nurse Joe and all the rest of them.

I haven't cried the entire time I've been cooped up in this place, but now I feel my eyes burn, and the cucumbers on my plate become blurry. It's just so . . . STUPID! My parents don't force me to eat cucumbers at home.

163

Why do I have to eat them here? How is being forced to eat a vegetable that I hate supposed to cure me of bulimia? It's bad enough having to follow the rules when they make sense — but this makes absolutely NO sense. It's nonsensical, ridiculous, stupid, and, above all, unjust. It makes me mad. It makes me crazy. It makes me . . . cry.

Tom gives my knee a comforting pat under the table — which I bet is against the fucking rules, too — but it just makes me cry more. I can barely see my tray as I stab at the rest of the salad, eating my way around the offending cukes. Tears drip from my chin onto the tray as I shovel the Jell-O down my throat, one spoonful after another, until the container is empty. And then it's just me and the cucumbers, and I just *cannot* and *will not eat them*. Nor will I drink that disgusting Ensure stuff. They can make me sit here all night tonight and all day tomorrow and the whole night and day after that, but I'm not going to give in because it's just STUPID STUPID STUPID and SO *INCREDIBLY* UNFAIR.

"Come on, Janie. You can do it. Just hold your nose and down the hatch," Tom says.

"No. I'm *not going to*."

I know I sound like a Terrible Two-year-old in the middle of a tantrum, but that's kind of how I feel being forced to stay at the table until I eat those gross, disgusting things.

"Tom, if you're finished, you can leave the table," Nurse Kay says.

"It's okay. I'll stay here and keep Janie company."

"Me, too," Missy adds.

I smile at her gratefully through my tears, because I know what a sacrifice it is for her, not to be able to pace around during that awful post-meal pukeless half hour.

"Actually, I need you both to leave the table now," Nurse Kay says.

"What, we're not even allowed to give Janie moral support?" Missy explodes. "That's bullshit! That's almost as bullshit as making her eat those fricking cucumbers instead of extra tomatoes!"

"Missy. Leave the table NOW," Nurse Kay, whom I now totally hate, orders through gritted teeth. "You, too, Tom."

"This is complete and total crap," Missy mutters as she gets up. She picks up her tray and slams it into the tray return.

"Hang in there, Janie," Tom whispers as he slides out of his chair.

It's just me and two of the Starvers, Tracey and Bethany, left at the table. Eventually, even they finish, and it's just me, the cucumbers, and that witch, Nurse Kay. I don't know how I ever thought she was nice.

She sits down across the table from me.

"Janie, you need to eat your cucumbers and get this over with. It can't be all *that* bad."

I sit there, tears streaming down my face, staring at the evil green slices on my tray. Now I know how Harry feels when my mother is trying to make him eat broccoli or asparagus. She always uses the "it can't be that bad" line when he starts gagging. I used to think she was right, but now I understand that's just because I *like* aspar-agus and broccoli. I never understood that for Harry, who's an incredibly picky eater, every meal is like being in Golden Slopes with a tray of cucumbers in front of you. The poor kid.

As I sit there crying, ignoring Nurse Kay and refusing to eat, I realize that it's not about the vegetable; the cucumber's just what got me started. It's about the irrational unfairness of it all. It's about having to wait for all the Starvers to come to the table when I'm starving myself. It's about being denied phone and visitor privileges because of purging into my sock. It's about the fact that my family will never forgive me for ruining Perfect Jenny's wedding day — and I'll never be able to forgive myself. It's about Matt Lewis dumping me, Kelsey being mad at me for not telling her I was bulimic, and the look on Danny's face when he saw me crying hysterically on the bathroom floor with puke spatter on my bridesmaid's dress. It's about the fact that my father will never think I'm as perfect as Jenny, and my mother will be perpetually disappointed that I don't measure up. It's about hating who I am and the way I look and what's become of my life after a mere sixteen years of living it. It's about feeling mad and sad and confused and miserable and angry and having all those emotions swirling around in my head and my stomach and wanting to purge them away but knowing I'm going to have to sit at this table until kingdom come unless I eat these *goddamn cucumbers.*

Nurse Kay sighs and gets up from the table.

"I have to go distribute meds," she says. "But Joe is going to come and sit with you until you're finished."

She goes to the door and calls down to the nurses' station for Joe to take over the role of Food Führer.

I throw down my fork in protest, push back my chair from the table, and fold my arms across my chest. If they think GI Joe can sweet-talk me into eating those damn things, they've got another think coming.

"What's up, Janie?" Joe says, taking the chair across from me, turning it around and straddling it. "Why all the fuss about a few little cucumbers?"

"Because I HATE them, that's why! And it's totally stupid that I should have to eat them when I've offered to eat double the amount of tomato or mushrooms or peppers or some other vegetable that I *do* like."

Joe takes a deep breath and leans his elbows on the back of the chair.

"Look, Janie, I'm not going to pretend to you that I understand the reason for making you eat cucumbers. But there are rules in every institution and organization. Heck, you think this is bad? You should try being in the Marines."

"I don't give a shit about the frickin' Marines," I shout. "I just DON'T WANT TO EAT THESE GODDAMN CUCUMBERS!"

I burst into another round of angry sobs.

"Whoa, take it easy there, sport. Don't lose control of yourself over something small like this."

Something *small*? He just doesn't get it. Nobody gets it. Nobody gets *me*. I don't think anyone ever will. I'm overwhelmed with despair — after weeks of not being able to cry, now I feel like I'll never be able to stop, the sadness is so huge.

Joe hands me a box of tissues and just sits across the table without saying a word.

I'm just crying and crying, soaking through tissue after tissue. Half an hour passes, but I don't even see Joe look at his watch. I wish he would get up and go to the bathroom so I could throw the freakin' cukes in the garbage and be done with this, but Joe seems to have infinite patience, not to mention an ironclad bladder.

Finally he says, "You know, Janie, if you just get those cucumbers down the hatch, I promise to take you to the gym for a workout later on."

I want to go whale on that punching bag; I want it more than anything. But I can't do it unless I manage to swallow all six of those disgusting green discs on my tray.

Staring at them, I realize that I can't let myself be defeated by a small green vegetable, no matter how much I hate it. I just can't.

You know those bumper stickers *"What would Jesus do?"* As I'm sitting there crying, I start to think about that. Since I'm Jewish, Jesus isn't a person I feel comfortable asking for help, as great a guy as he might have been. Let's see . . . I know, what would Moses do? Well, Moses had a direct line to God. He'd probably just tap the cucumbers with his staff and they'd turn into chocolate éclairs or French fries or something more palatable. Scratch that.

What would Dad do? He'd round up a group of investors and launch a hostile takeover of Golden Slopes, buy the place, and change their ridiculous cucumber policy.

Mom? She'd start crying, but I'm already doing that and it doesn't seem to be having much impact on any of the hard-hearted Food Nazis in this joint. Or she'd go into intensive OCD cleaning mode, organizing the out-of-date magazines in the dayroom by title and publication date. Failing that, she'd go shopping.

Since I can't leave the table, the OCD option isn't open to me. And there ain't a whole lot to buy in the lockup ward at Golden Slopes other than cans of Ensure.

Jenny? I bet you anything Jenny would never be stuck in this position. She'd be sitting here asking for *extra* cucumbers.

Which leaves my little brother — what would Harry do? And then it strikes me: If Harry doesn't like something, he just smothers it in ketchup, which drowns out the taste of whatever he's put it on.

"Joe," I sniff, "could I have some ketchup . . . please?"

"Coming right up," he says, handing me a bunch of ketchup packets from the condiment tray.

I pour ketchup all over the offending vegetables, so that not one iota of green is visible. Then I fork one and put it in my mouth. The texture is still gross and cucumbery, but at least the taste is predominantly ketchup, so I can get the thing down. It takes five minutes, and I find myself gagging once or twice, but thanks to the Harry method, I manage to clean my tray.

Joe inspects the tray, my napkin, my lap, and the floor around me, to make sure I haven't surreptitiously managed to dispose of a slice or two.

"Okay, Janie, you're free to leave. Go do your half hour in with the rest of them, then I'll pick you up in about forty-five minutes to go to the gym. You can ask if anyone else wants to head over there with us."

I feel like dancing, even though I'm still crying,

because I'm free to leave. I wish I were free to walk out the door and go home, but right now it feels good just to get up from the table and spend a half hour reading old *People* magazines.

Callie, Missy, and Tom are waiting for me. They surround me and give me a group hug, even though it's against the rules.

"That so completely SUCKED!" Missy says.

"How'd you manage?" Callie asks.

I laugh through my tears and pose the question that "saved" me: "What would Harry do?"

"O . . . *kay*," Missy says. "What the hell is *that* supposed to mean?"

"I would guess . . . maybe it's like *What would Jesus do?*" Tom says. "Is that right, Janie?"

"Got it first guess." I smile at him. "And the answer is . . . ketchup!"

We spend the next half hour asking each other "What would X do" questions, like "What would George Washington do?" or "What would Harry Potter do?"

I might have known these people only a short time, but it's like we know more about each other than we do about most of our friends on the "outside." There's something about spilling your guts in group, taking off your mask and admitting to the real depth of your pain, that accelerates the pace of friendship. I wonder if it stays that way when you leave this place. I sure as hell hope so.

CHAPTER 12

August 2nd

Crying over cukes must have done something (Cucumber Catharsis?) because I'm seriously thinking about talking to Dr. Pardy about everything. Tom says I should give her a chance to help me, but I don't know. I'm scared — well, petrified, more like it. I'm afraid she'll just tell everything to my parents and then it'll be even worse with them than it is already. But I'm going to think about it some more. Maybe I'll score brownie points for letting her fish in my troubled psyche and that'll help me get out of here sooner. And I REALLY WANT TO GET OUT OF HERE!

August 3rd

Tom came out to his parents yesterday in a meeting with Dr. Pardy. He looked like he'd been twenty rounds with the world heavyweight champ when he came out of it, let me tell you. I was dying to know how it went but he said, "I'll talk to you later, Janie, okay?" Then he went to his room and slept for two hours.

The suspense was practically killing me. When he finally came into the dayroom, I grabbed him, dragged him over to the comfy chairs in the corner, and ordered him to spill.

When he did, I almost wished I hadn't. Can you believe this? His dad, the lying, cheating, insensitive jerk, said, "If I'd known you were going to turn out gay, I would have made your mother have an abortion."

I swear to G-d, some people just shouldn't be allowed to procreate. Seriously! What kind of father would say something like that to his kid? It makes my dad saying my acting isn't important look like nothing at all, and you know how upset I was about that.

Apparently Tom's mom went ballistic when his Dad said that, and I don't blame her. I'd want to beat the crap out of whoever said something like that about my kid.

Tom's mom might not have done that, but she came back last night about half an hour before visiting hours ended and told Tom that she'd asked his dad for a divorce. It's funny because with all the fighting my parents were doing about Jenny's wedding, I've spent a lot of time freaking out that they were going to get divorced. To me, the idea of my parents splitting up is like the end of the world.

But Tom seemed almost happy about it — at least in the beginning. Well, maybe happy is stretching it, but definitely relieved. But then he started feeling guilty, like that it was his announcing that he was gay that destroyed his parents' marriage. I don't know what Dr. Pardy told him (he's been spending a lot of time closeted — hahaha — in her office), but I know what I said. And that's that I think he did his mom a favor. It seems to me like she was trapped in this crappy, unhappy marriage but didn't have the . . . I don't know . . . courage? Maybe that's not the right word, but basically she didn't know how to get out of it. I told Tom that maybe it took his dad saying something that godawful about his kid to give her the excuse she needed to make a change.

I mean, I know how I would feel. At least I think I do. It's one thing for someone to be a jerk to me. That's bad enough. But if someone ever did to Kelsey what Matt Lewis did to me, I swear, I'd want to tear him limb from limb.

Back when Harry was in second grade, some fourth grader was being mean to him when they were walking home from the bus stop. He didn't want to tell Mom or Dad because he knew Mom would totally freak out and Dad would do something over the top like suing the kid's parents. Harry only told me because I happened to be the one who was home when he walked in, practically in tears, and I just nagged him until he told me what was up. When he did, I felt this whole Mama Bear thing welling up, even though he's my younger brother and not my kid. I felt like beating the crap out of the little punk who was bullying him. The jerk was violating the Law of the Older Sibling, namely that I'm the only one who's allowed to be mean to my little brother.

So the next day, I went to meet Harry at the bus stop, and when he pointed out the kid who'd been hassling him, I went up to the twerp and told him what I would do to him if he ever dared to even look at my brother the wrong way. Harry didn't have trouble with the idiot again.

All I'm saying is that a lot of times it's easier to fight for someone else than it is for your-self. At least that's the way it is for me. I don't know why. I mean, I know that other people shouldn't be treated badly. So why do I put up with it myself?

I don't just have butterflies as I knock on the door of Dr. Pardy's office the next day — I've got the entire Butterfly Garden at the Bronx Zoo fluttering in my stomach.

"Come on in," she calls. "Make yourself comfortable."

Comfortable is about the last thing I can make myself right now, but I sit in one of the comfy chairs, kick off my shoes, and sit cross-legged, trying to give myself some advantage.

"What's on your mind, Janie?"

Talk about a loaded question.

"I . . . well . . . I . . ."

And then, without my having any control over it, I burst into tears. The stupid thing is, I don't even know why I'm crying. I don't even know why I'm sitting in Dr. Pardy's office, what I expect her to be able to do for me, how she can possibly help. All I do know is that I'm sick of feeling this way. I hate being the way I am. I'm sick of being sad, I'm sick of feeling angry. I want things to be different, better, but I just don't know how to make it happen.

After blowing through half of one of the ever-present boxes of tissues, I end up telling Dr. Pardy about the mandala.

"It's been bumming me out ever since we did that stupid mandala thing in art therapy. Because . . ."

Dammit, I've started crying again.

"Because I don't know what to put in the middle. Because I don't know who I am. Trying to do that mandala made me realize I've got this . . . huge . . . black hole inside me."

Dr. Pardy waits patiently while I blow my nose, loudly, a couple of times.

"Janie, from where I sit, you are a lovely, bright, caring, sensitive young woman. Your parents tell me that you're an honor student and an extremely talented actress."

"Yeah, right. You heard my dad. He said that play practice isn't important. I don't even think he *sees* me most of the time. He just sees his *idea* of me."

"Well, I think we were at the same meeting and what I understood your father to say was that he doesn't think play practice is as important as you getting well, not that he doesn't think it's important, period," Dr. Pardy says.

"But . . . it's important to *me*," I sniff. "Weird as it sounds, it's only when I'm playing someone else that I feel like I'm really me."

"That takes me back to your feeling about the 'black hole' inside," Dr. Pardy says. "The thing is, Janie, you can't count on other people to fill up that black hole. It's mostly up to you. Sure, family and friends contribute something — maybe they might fill ten percent or so, fifteen if you're really lucky and have a very supportive family or are fortunate enough to have a network of terrific friends."

"Yeah, you know what they say: 'You can't pick your family, but you *can* pick your friends.'"

"It's true — sometimes when a family situation is destructive to one's mental health, it's possible to create a supportive family of friends," says Dr. Pardy. "But the point I'm making here is that the major work in filling what you call the 'black hole' is up to you."

"But how? All I know is that it's there. I don't have a clue how to fill it up."

"I can't tell you how to do it, Janie, other than it's about answering this question: *Who is Janie Ryman?* Not who Janie's dad thinks she is, or who Janie's mom thinks she is, or even who Janie's *friends* think she is. No, the question is what makes you, *Janie,* tick. That's one of the reasons we do the mandala exercise at Golden Slopes. To get you started on the process of being able to answer that question."

She gets up from behind her desk and comes to sit on the sofa across from me.

"But I can tell you one thing for certain, Janie.

Bingeing isn't going to fill that hole for you. It might feel that way temporarily. But it won't do the job."

"And it makes me feel like crap afterward," I admit.

"And causes you to damage your teeth, your esophagus, and your bones, not to mention putting you at risk of dying," Dr. Pardy adds.

Wow. Thanks for reminding me of those cheerful facts when I'm already well and truly miserable.

"Janie, I've got some homework for you," she says.

Doesn't Dr. Pardy realize this is supposed to be my summer vacation? Jeez. Although seriously, I can think of about a zillion places I'd rather be spending my summer vacation than Golden Slopes.

"What's that?"

Although my lack of enthusiasm couldn't be more obvious, Dr. P is either oblivious or chooses to ignore it.

"Since you seem to enjoy journaling, I'd like you to write about the crisis that precipitated your hospitalization," she says. "And then I'd really like you to share it in group tomorrow . . . assuming you feel comfortable doing so."

She has *got* to be kidding. I don't even think I can write about that, much less stand up in front of a bunch of people in group and read the whole sorry story aloud.

"I don't know, I . . ."

"Try, Janie. I think it's really important that you try."

I take a tissue, do a last nose blow, and reluctantly tell her I will.

When I open the door to my room, I surprise Callie and catch her carving something on her leg with the end of a paper clip. It looks incredibly painful, and I know she shouldn't be doing it. I don't even know how she got hold of a paper clip — it's all about keeping us from trying to kill ourselves in here: no belts, no shoelaces, no real mirrors except in the vitals room where they weigh us in, take our temperature and blood pressure, and check our bodies for attempts at self-harm — like trying to carve stuff on your leg with a paper clip.

"Callie — what the hell are you *doing*? You're going to get in trouble for doing that!"

She draws the end of the paper clip across her thigh, leaving a thin trail of blood in its wake, and mimics me:

"*You're going to get in trouble for doing that!* Like I'm supposed to give a shit about that."

"But *why*? Why are you doing that to yourself?"

"What do *you* care?"

"Because I'm your *friend*. Because I don't want you to hurt yourself like that."

Callie laughs unpleasantly. "My *friend*? You don't even *know* me. You don't even know a *fraction* of what my life is about. So why don't you go find your little fairy friend and worry about him instead?"

Why the hell does she have to bring *that* into the discussion?

"Do me a favor — leave Tom out of this. I thought you of all people would be more sensitive and respectful."

"What do you mean by that?" she says, drawing more blood from her leg. I can't stand to even look at what she's doing — how can she do it to herself? "Me *of all people*? Why me of all people? Because I'm such a freak myself?"

"No — I don't think you're a freak. Not at all. I guess because you're different, too. I would think you know how he feels."

"Different. That's just a polite way of saying freak. So listen, Miss Goody Two-Shoes — why don't you get your perfect little self out of here and leave me alone, okay?"

Me? *Perfect?* In what universe might *that* be?

I don't want to leave Callie alone, because I don't want her to keep hurting herself. But short of wrestling the paper clip away from her — and Callie's a lot bigger and stronger than I am — I don't know what else to do.

I grab my journal and a pen and head for the door.

"I was just trying to help. To be a friend. I'm sorry if that offends you so much."

I slam the door behind me.

Once I'm in the hallway, I don't know what to do. I don't want Callie to end up like Helen — not that she'd be able to kill herself with a paper clip. But even in the two and a half weeks I've known her she's changed — and not for the better. She's angrier, bitchier, yet at the same time . . . almost, I don't know . . . detached. Like the way she was just sitting there and hurting herself, watching the blood well up from her skin like she didn't feel the pain. Or she didn't even care if she did.

Part of me wants to take her at her word and just leave her alone to do whatever she wants to herself. I mean, it's her body, isn't it? If she wants to do weird shit to it, then that's her problem.

But there's another part of me, the part I wish I could ignore, that tells me if I care about Callie, that if I want to really be a good friend to her — to help her — I need to tell a nurse about what I just saw, even though I'm worried that Callie will beat the crap out of me for doing so.

Unfortunately, that part wins out. Instead of heading for the dayroom to write, I make my way to the nurses' station.

"Um, Nurse Kay?"

"Yes, Janie, how can I help?"

"Can I tell you something . . . in private?"

The last thing I want is for anyone to witness me being a stool pigeon.

"Sure," she says, coming out from behind the desk. "Rose, cover for me, will you?"

She leads me into the vitals room.

"So what's up?"

"Well . . . I wasn't sure what to do . . . I mean, if I should tell you because I don't want to get anyone in trouble but . . . well, when I went into my room just now, Callie was hurting herself."

It's like someone flips a switch inside Nurse Kay — all of a sudden she's in emergency mode, all brisk, business-like, and to the point.

"How exactly?"

"She's carving stuff on her leg with a paper clip. I mean, I don't think she's trying to kill herself or anything, but . . . well, it looked pretty painful. Except it didn't seem like she was actually feeling the pain."

"Okay, Janie, thanks for letting me know."

She opens the door to the vitals room and herds me out.

"And, Janie . . ."

"Yes?"

"You did the right thing by telling me — I know it couldn't have been easy."

She practically runs down the hallway toward our room, and I make my escape to the dayroom.

CHAPTER THIRTEEN

August 4th

I've already written about how I first met Matt Lewis back in middle school, and how I had a crush on him ever since. How I watched him go out with a seemingly never-ending procession of girls at school, and always dreamed that I would be one of them. No, scratch that. Not one of them. The One. *I thought one day he would wake up and realize that although there were girls that were prettier than me, that were thinner than me, that had better breasts and better thighs and better hair and better, well, pretty much everything, that I was the one that he really loved and wanted.*

Listen, I'm writing this in a psychiatric hospital, so I'm not saying this hope was entirely rational. In fact, I'm not saying it was rational at all, and what happened certainly proved that point. *But it was what I'd hoped for, what I'd fantasized about when he was my lab partner in science class, what*

I'd had hot dreams about at night on a pretty regular basis.

So is it any wonder that when he walked into the cast party the night of my triumphant performance as Anne Frank, I felt my heartbeat go into overdrive? And because I was still high from the applause — from receiving my first standing ovation from an audience — I felt confident enough to flirt with him. There was something about having played Anne and played her well that made me feel worthy and special . . . even beautiful.

Everything seemed magical that night. Matt putting his arm around me as people kept coming up and telling me how awesome I'd been. Matt kissing my hair and whispering in my ear about how he wanted to get me alone. Him taking me by the hand and leading me upstairs into an empty bedroom, closing the door and kissing me, nibbling my lips and pressing his body against me. Matt reaching under my shirt and unhooking my bra and . . . well, I'm not going to go on and on like one of those trashy romance novels, but I felt like I had died and gone to heaven, making out with him in that bedroom. He wanted to go further, of course, but even though I'd worshiped him for years, I wasn't about to do that the first time he kissed me, even though I was tempted. Oh, my G-d, how I was tempted!

"Maybe next time," I said. Because I wanted there to be a next time, of course.

"Yeah, maybe we can catch a movie next

weekend or something," he whispered, making one last attempt to get his hand into my jeans.

I grabbed his hand. "Next time."

At school the next week I was practically floating on air. Sure, I had to deal with the annoyance of the Mattettes hanging all over my man, but still — when he kissed me in the middle of the courtyard in front of any number of girls who were way prettier and thinner than me, it didn't seem to matter.

Mom wanted me to stay home for dinner with Jenny and Brad the following Saturday night, but there was no way I was going to give up a date with Matt to sit at home and listen to them all argue about last-minute wedding decisions.

"By the way, what table am I sitting at next week?" I asked, looking over Jenny's shoulder at the seating chart, which looked like the Rosetta Stone, there were so many names crossed out and scribbled in. "It had better be the same one as Matt Lewis."

"Well, it isn't," snapped Jenny, who I thought must be suffering from a serious case of prewedding jitters — or just being a bitch. "You're sitting at the head table with the rest of the wedding party."

"What?!" I protested. "C'mon, I don't want to be at the head table with all the geriatrics. I want to sit with Matt!"

"Eh-hem. At thirty-two, I'm still several decades away from AARP membership, thank you very much," Brad said, but at least he was smiling, which is more than I could say for Jenny.

"Janie, I cannot believe how selfish you are! Do you realize how many hours I've spent on this seating chart, so that none of the people who sided with Mom in the divorce have to sit near people who sided with Dad? Or so none of your *mother's* friends are seated with my *mother's* friends? Now you want me to change it all just so you can sit next to some guy?"

I wanted to tell her that Matt wasn't just "some guy" — he was my boyfriend, not to mention the hottest man on the planet. But I wasn't quite ready to go public with that information after just one week.

"Mom — can't you do anything about this?"

Mom gave me a Look.

"Janie, Jenny's right. You're being selfish. This has been stressful enough for her" (I could almost hear her thinking, "and me") "and you need to be thinking about how to help her, not giving her more to worry about."

Et tu, *Mom?*

"Well, I'll just get my selfish butt out of here — I'm going to the movies. Bye!"

I slammed the door on the way out for good measure.

Matt was going to pick me up at home, but I walked to the end of the driveway to meet him, because I couldn't stand another minute with the Wedding Zombies. Plus, I was kind of nervous about my parents knowing that Matt and I were dating. Why? you might ask. . . . Because wasn't he *every father's wet dream when it came to boyfriend material? Smart, good-looking, from a good family ("we know the parents and they're fine people"), and clearly headed for a stellar — and lucrative — career in finance.*

But that was it — I was worried that it would make my parents too *happy. Okay, I can hear you saying . . . but isn't making your parents — particularly your dad — as happy as Perfect Jenny does, what you obsess about constantly? Well, yeah. But the thing is, if I told them about Matt and then something went wrong — as it did, so spectacularly — then I would be the one to blame. Because a fine boy like Matt couldn't possibly have fucked it up. No, if something went wrong, it would almost certainly be because I, Janie, the black sheep of the Ryman family, had done something to make it so. And, sure enough, that's how it played out.*

Back to that night — Matt picked me up and I thought we were going to the movies, but instead he said, "Hey, my folks are having dinner at the country club. Why don't we head back to my place for a swim?"

"But I don't have a bathing suit," I protested.

He just grinned at me.

I was completely freaking out the whole way there. I couldn't skinny dip (or in my case "fat dip") with Matt Lewis. He'd see all my blubber and be disgusted and he'd never want to see me again.

To say that I was feeling sick with nerves when

we got to his house is a major understatement. I wanted to purge, desperately.

Matt took my hand and kissed me when I got out of the car. I wanted to relax, to enjoy the sensation of being in his arms and his fantastic kisses, but I was too busy imagining the look of revulsion on his face when he saw my body.

He led me to the pool house — which was really more of a pool mansion, with marble bathroom, kitchen, big-screen TV, and huge, comfortable sofa.

"I could quite happily live in your pool house," I said.

He laughed. "You're not the first one who's said that."

Argh. He thought I was predictable. Boring.

"Do you want a beer?" he asked.

"Um . . . okay."

I figured it would loosen me up. Make me feel less self-conscious. Although it would also make me bloat. So that was my choice: Loosen up and bloat or freak out and . . .

I drank the beer. When Matt took off his shirt and started to unbutton mine, I asked him for another. I asked for a third when he took his hands off my breasts and unzipped his pants.

By the time he had my jeans off and said, "Let's take a dip in the pool first," my head was spinning. It's not like I'd never drank before, don't get me wrong, but I'd never had three beers *in quick succession like that. And boy, it worked on the loosening-up front. When I dove into the pool (I kept on my bra and bikini underwear because I just couldn't do the Full Monty thing, and Matt kept on his boxers, thank goodness), I wasn't even conscious of my belly being bloated by carbs — I felt like this underwater sea nymph, floating through the depths, admiring his tight, washboard abs and the way the wet boxers clung to Matt's butt and thighs. Clearly, beer bloat doesn't affect golden gods like Matt Lewis. We splashed and frolicked and made out and then he said, "Let's go get another beer," and he led me back into the pool house and handed me a huge fluffy towel to dry off, which was great because I could cover up my beer belly with it.*

I was still feeling kind of dizzy and my stomach was churning with beer? Nerves? All of the above?

"I need to use the restroom," I said.

My legs were pretty wobbly as I made my way to the bathroom, which was completely marbled with gold-plated taps and stuff. I couldn't believe that people would actually spend that much money to make a pool house bathroom that plush. I turned on the water in the sink so Matt wouldn't hear me heaving and stuck my fingers down my throat. I figured if I puked up some of the beer, maybe I wouldn't feel so drunk and I'd have a flatter stomach having barfed up all those carbs.

I found some toothpaste in the medicine cabinet over the sink and brushed my teeth with my finger. There were several bottles of expensive-looking perfume sitting on the counter and I choose one and spritzed it around my head to take away any lingering vomit smell.

Matt handed me another beer as soon as I sat down, and pulled the towel away.

"You smell like my mother," he said as he leaned in to kiss me.

Great. Not quite the effect I was going for, but I guessed smelling like his mother was marginally better than smelling like puke, even if it might be a little . . . I don't know, Oedipal.

Matt unhooked my bra and I tensed up, because as much as I liked him, I was afraid. Afraid to let him see all of me because he might not like what he saw, afraid that if he did like what he saw that he'd want to go further. Afraid that he'd find out that I was a virgin.

I'm sure I wasn't the only virgin at Pine Ridge High, but I was equally sure that with all the girls Matt had to choose from, he wouldn't be that interested in dating one.

"Have some more beer," he said. "You seem a little tense."

And here I was supposed to be such a good actress. I'd have to pretend I'm playing the part of a sexy, experienced kinda gal, I thought. So I chugged the rest of my beer, and then wrapped my arms around Matt's neck and kissed him.

We were at it hot and heavy when I felt his hand reach down to pull off my wet underpants.

"Matt, I . . ."

"Oh, baby, you're so hot," he said.

What could I say to that?

But when he pulled down his wet boxers and I saw him, all erect, I was scared and confused. I'd worshiped the guy for years — but when I'd pictured losing my virginity, it definitely was a more romantic scenario than being drunk on a pool house sofa, even if it was a very ritzy pool house.

"Matt, I need to . . ."

"Don't worry, I've got it covered, baby."

From somewhere, I don't know where, he magicked up a condom and put it on.

"But, Matt, I . . ."

"Don't back out on me now, Janie," he said, kissing me as he rolled on top of me and started poking between my thighs. "C'mon, baby."

I didn't want to. I mean, I might have wanted my first time to be with Matt Lewis, but I wanted it to be something more than this. But I did it anyway. And it hurt like anything.

Afterward, when I went into the bathroom to clean up the blood from my thighs, I cried. I thought I would feel so close and wonderful when I had sex with someone, but I didn't. I felt sad and empty and really lonely.

"I can't believe you were a virgin," Matt said. "I wish you'd told me so I could have put a towel down. There's blood on the sofa. My mother is going to be really pissed, and I'm not sure how I'm supposed to explain it to her."

I'd just given my virginity to the guy and all he could think about was how he was going explain the stain on the sofa to his mother. This was so NOT how I imagined it would be.

I got dressed after that, because I felt so exposed and vulnerable. I balled my wet underpants and bra up and shoved them in my purse. "I'd better get home," I said. "My mom was pretty pissed I went out in the first place, what with the wedding coming up next week."

"Yeah. The wedding. My parents said we have to go to that. You in the wedding party?"

"Of course. And I've got to wear this awful yellow dress. I swear, when I get married, I'm going to let my bridesmaids wear whatever the hell they like. I'm not going to turn into some awful Bridezilla like Jenny."

He slapped my butt.

"Well, let's get you home. Don't want to get Mrs. R even more mad."

And that was how I lost my virginity to Matt Lewis. Pretty anticlimactic, if you'll excuse the pun.

I didn't see him the following week because school was over and I was forced to do all this wedding shit. The next time I saw him was at the wedding. . . .

So I've already written about how Kelsey came to visit the morning after the wedding and about how I was a total asshole to her. After Kelsey left, I lay in bed wondering if life could get any worse. My stomach churned, the little men with jackhammers continued to chip away at the inside of my skull, and a continuous loop of the painful, humiliating, and catastrophic events of the night before played in my brain. I hadn't just fucked up Perfect Jenny's wedding, the big day that every girl dreams about. I hadn't just embarrassed my entire family. I hadn't just done something most people would have considered impossible, namely created even more friction between Mom, Dad, and Clarissa. That trifecta of wrongdoing was just the tip of the iceberg. In less than twenty-four hours, I'd screwed up Jenny's wedding, ensured that I'd be grounded for the rest of my natural life, and condemned myself to a life of unremitting humiliation. It was hard to imagine that the day before I'd woken up with so much hope and anticipation, picturing myself dancing the night away in Matt's arms. Ha!

I decided to try and take a shower, to see if I could wash away the self-revulsion, as if being under a stream of steaming hot water could somehow rid me of the feeling that I was dirty and loathsome.

Groaning, I sat up and swung my legs over the side of the bed. It made my head spin as well as thump, and I thought the combination would make me throw up again. Quickly, I lowered my head down between my legs and tried to take a few deep breaths. It felt like my brain was a kettledrum being played by someone holding a serious grudge. Not that I didn't deserve it.

When the room finally stopped spinning, I shuffled to the bathroom. I locked the door and turned the shower on to the hottest setting while I got undressed.

One thing I've hated about my bathroom is that there are so many mirrors. I used to think it was cool when I was a kid, because I could see so many different angles of myself. But now it just gives me more ways to hate my body. I've learned to start the shower on the hottest setting the minute I get into the bathroom so that the mirrors will be all steamed up by the time I have to take my clothes off.

But before my features were hidden by the merciful steam, I caught a glimpse of my bloodshot eyes and swollen eyelids and I hated the Janie I saw looking back at me — I hated her with a passion. Judging by the expression on her face, it was pretty clear she hated me, too.

When I was finally unable to see myself other than as a faint outline, I peeled off my pajamas and stepped into the shower. The water was so hot it almost burned my skin but I didn't care. I needed to feel pain. I deserved to feel pain... because maybe if I felt enough physical pain, I would stop feeling so much pain inside.

After a few minutes I felt dizzy and I leaned my forehead against the shower's cool, tiled wall, staring down at the water as it washed off my hideous, fat body and circled the drain below.

I don't know how long I stood like that, because I shut my eyes and tried very hard not to think. First I tried not to think of the fist I felt in my stomach when I first caught a glimpse of Matt Lewis flirting with my cousin Haley, who was wearing some slinky, strapless number, while I was stuck sitting at the head table in my hideous lemon dress. Then I tried not to think but couldn't help remembering how disbelief crept over my whole body like a thousand fire ants, disbelief that my guy, the guy to whom I'd given my virginity a mere seven days before, was now smiling that same intimate "you're the most beautiful girl in my world" smile at cousin Haley. I tried to forget how I reached for Brad's cousin's champagne glass and downed it in one gulp as I watched Haley flirt back. How I hated my cousin with a sudden, fierce rage because she was flirting with my guy, even though deep down I knew she had no way of knowing that he was mine, or at least that I thought he was. I tried not to remember how I shoveled two entire pieces of wedding cake into my mouth in short succession when I saw Matt take Haley's hand and lead her onto the parquet floor and then washed them down with another glass of champagne as the two of them started dancing, slowly, sensuously, completely in synch, as if they were made to be together. I wanted to scream. I wanted to cry out, "Matt, how can you be looking at her the same way you looked at me?"

But instead I sat there at that stupid head table, feeling like molten lava shrouded in ice, unable to show how I felt because everyone was looking and some asshole with a video camera was asking me if I had a message for the newlyweds. I sat there hating Jenny for making me wear that awful yellow dress and not letting me sit with Matt, hating Haley for being prettier and skinnier and for looking so good in that goddamn slinky outfit, hating the way I looked and the way I felt. I hated the world, hated my life, hated myself. I tried to forget how I reached for yet another glass of champagne as Matt put his arms around Haley and pulled her body into his. I tried not to remember how his body felt next to mine in the pool house the week before. And most of all I tried to forget how his blond head dipped to kiss her bare shoulder, his hands, the same hands that had touched me so intimately only a week before, slid down her back to rest on her thin, shapely ass. It wasn't just my heart that shattered, but my entire, miserable, fucked-up world.

I tried not to remember knocking back a few more glasses of champagne as I sat surrounded by the fragments of everything I believed was true and right. The service at the Waterside really was impeccable, just like Clarissa said it would be. They kept filling Brad's cousin's glass every time I emptied it. After I'd downed the fifth glass of champagne, the cousin came back so I couldn't drink anymore, which was probably a good thing because right then Danny came up and asked me to dance. When I tried to get up, my head started spinning and I tripped on the edge of the dance floor, completely unsteady on high heels in combination with too much bubbly.

Danny grabbed my arm to keep me from falling. As hot water beat down on my back, I remembered the gentle look of concern as he asked me if I was okay, the way he put his arm around my waist to steady me, and it made me want to cry — but I couldn't. It was like I'd used up a lifetime's allotment of tears and there were none left to shed.

I tried not to remember what happened when over Danny's shoulder I saw Matt making out with Haley. I knew, completely and irrevocably, that I'd been used. What had been so special to me was just another fuck to Matt. I tried to forget how I wrenched myself out of Danny's arms and left him standing alone on the dance floor, how I ran out of the ballroom, past Jenny and Brad, past Dad who was dancing with Brad's mother, and Mom who was dancing with Brad's dad, past Kelsey who shouted, "Janie, what's the matter?" as I raced by, how I didn't stop until I'd made it to the safety of the ladies' lounge and locked myself in a stall, how I stuck my finger down my throat and out came a waterfall of canapés and loup de mer au vin blanc, chocolate wedding cake, and champagne. How it spattered into my hair and onto my outfit and how I didn't even care because I hated that hideous dress anyway.

I tried not to remember Kelsey banging on the stall door shouting, "Janie, are you all right? Open the damn door!" and refusing to go away until I obeyed. I tried really hard not to remember her shocked and horrified expression when she saw the puke on my dress and my chin and in my hair, and I especially tried to forget how I felt my stomach heave again and couldn't turn around fast enough and heaved up canapé-chocolate cake-champagne puke on the designer dress her mother had let her borrow with dire warnings about Kelsey's life expectancy if anything should happen to it.

I tried not to remember her shriek of dismay, me slumping onto the floor in a puddle of puke, crying my drunken apologies until snot came out of my nose. I told her about losing my virginity to Matt, about seeing him with Haley, and about being bulimic. I can't help remembering how surprised I was that she was really mad at me instead of being the understanding and sympathetic friend she normally was. I tried not to remember looking up and seeing Danny and wondering why the hell he was in the girls' bathroom, and then hearing one of Clarissa's friends screaming because there was a male in the ladies' lounge, and her asking Danny if he was some kind of pervert until she caught a glimpse of me. I tried not to remember my mother and Clarissa screaming at each other and at me, but most of all I tried to forget the sight of Perfect Jenny in her wedding gown, tears streaming down her face, crying, "Janie, how COULD you?" Because when they asked me if I was sick, I had to tell them the truth, that I had done all this to myself.

I felt something dripping down my face, and I thought I'd finally managed to cry, but when I opened my eyes and looked down I saw blood dripping, drip, drop, splat, onto the shower floor. Great, another nosebleed. Normally, I would have got out of the shower and stuffed some toilet paper up my nostril to make it stop, but I just stood there and watched, drop, splat, drip as blood continued to flow out of my nose. I watched it hit the tiles bright red and then fade to pink as it swirled its way into the drain.

I wanted to follow it into nothingness. I wanted myself to be able to disappear down the drain. I wanted to never have to face anyone ever again — most of all me.

That's when I decided to do it — the thing that got me put in here. Yeah, I know I've been making out like it was just the bulimia that got me in here, but I've been lying to you — and to myself, in a way.

What earned me my one-way ticket to Golden Slopes was the decision I made as I stood there under the hot spray watching my blood fade into pink oblivion. I ended up here because I got out of the shower, threw on a clean pair of pajamas, and snuck into my parents' bathroom, where I knew my mother had a bottle of Xanax, prescribed to help her get through "Wedding Stress." I ended up here because I went into my bedroom and swallowed *them all, then lay down on my bed thinking about how much better off everyone would be with me gone. Thinking about how much better off I would be with me gone, because when I was dead, I could finally stop hating myself.*

I only know what happened next from what the doctor told me when I came to on a gurney in the hospital emergency room after they'd pumped my stomach — or so I'm told.

"You almost died, young lady," he said, sternly. "You can thank your younger brother for the fact that you're alive."

Harry? *I thought, still woozy from all the Xanax in my system.* Harry *saved my life?*

"When he told your parents something was wrong with you because you wouldn't wake up and they wouldn't believe him because they thought you were just sleeping it off, your brother called 911."

Harry?! Harry called 911 even though my parents said I was okay? I bet Dad was ready to beat the crap out of him when the ambulance showed up.

"He's a brave young man, that brother of yours. I hope you thank him for saving you."

Yeah, I'll thank him all right, *I thought.* I'll thank him right before I kill him, because if I'd wanted to be saved, I wouldn't have taken all the fricking pills in the first place.

But there I go telling fibs again. If I'm going to be really honest with you — and myself — I'm glad

199

that Harry called 911. Even though life is certainly going to be no picnic, especially when I get out of here and have to face people — and worst of all go back to school, where no doubt the entire world has heard about Crazy Insaney Janie — I actually feel a little bit of hope. Maybe someday things are going to get better for me. Maybe I might be able to deal with things without sticking my fingers down my throat. Maybe I might actually learn how to speak up when I'm upset about things instead of stuffing my feelings and eating to distract myself from feeling them. Not so long ago, I would have laughed in your face if you'd said that to me. But now I see a glimmer of light in the black tunnel of my future. I see this strange something that I'd forgotten about. I think it's called possibility.

CHAPTER FOURTEEN

No one says anything right away after I finish reading the journal entry. Great . . . here I've disclosed the most humiliating and painful experiences of my life, and no one's got anything to say. I knew I shouldn't have listened to Dr. Pardy about sharing. . . .

But then Tom says, "What an asshole!"

"What do you expect? He's a *guy*," says Missy.

"What the hell is that supposed to mean?" Royce says. "Like girls don't ever cheat on their boyfriends?"

"I bet a girl wouldn't take a guy's virginity and then start making out with someone else in front of him — at a wedding, no less!" Missy retorts.

I think she's got a point there.

"So what did your dad say when you told him what happened?" Tracey asks.

"Are you *crazy*? I didn't tell my parents."

"But why ever *not*?" Tracey asks. "If you were my daughter, I'd sure want to know if someone had treated you so badly."

"Besides, why do *they* think you tried to kill your-self?" Bethany asks.

I give a bitter laugh.

"As far as they're concerned, my trying to kill myself is just another example of me being a drama queen and trying to get attention."

"But why don't you tell them the truth?" Tracey persists.

"Well, let's put it this way — I know if I told Dad, he'd want to go after Matt with a shotgun, and Mr. Lewis, Matt's dad, is one of his bigger clients. How am I supposed to put him in that position?"

"That's *bullshit*!" Missy explodes. "Your dad should totally care more about you than some client with a son who's a complete asshole."

"Exactly," Tracey agrees.

"But . . . you guys don't understand. My father's always held up Matt as this shining example of 'a fine young man' . . . like the kind of guy he hopes Harry will be one day."

To my horror, I feel a lump in my throat and my eyes fill up with tears; it's hard to believe that only a few days ago, P.C. (Pre-Cucumbers), they were as dry as the freakin' Sahara Desert.

"The thing is . . . I'm afraid that if I *do* tell them . . . that they'll blame me. They'll think it's all my fault . . . that *I* was the one who screwed things up, because . . . I'm s-such a godawful f-fuckup."

And then it's like a wall falling down, and I'm sobbing. I've finally shone a flashlight into that dark, frightening place, where my deepest fears hide — the fear that ultimately my parents won't believe me, that they'll think it's just me being "dramatic," and, most scary of all, that they won't love me.

Tom hands me a box of tissues.

"I really think you should tell them," he says. "Take it from me . . . even if they do react badly — like my dad did — at least you *know* how it's going to go down, instead of obsessing about all the awful things that *might* happen."

"It's important to remember that every relationship we have — be it parents, friends, spouses, lovers — every single relationship we enter into entails risk," says Dr. Pardy. "Sure it's a risk for you, Janie, to tell your parents the real reasons why you reacted the way you did at your sister's wedding, and why you felt hopeless enough about your future to overdose on your mother's Xanax. But if you aren't willing to even try to explain to them, they'll continue to stick with their own ideas for why they *think* you did it, which might have nothing to do with the true reasons."

"Like I said, I'd want to know about this if you were *my* daughter," Tracey says.

"It's also important for another reason," says Dr. Pardy. "The only way you are going to be able to learn and grow is to put these issues on the table where they can be seen and discussed, instead of trying to submerge them. Otherwise, they'll just continue to run you around in other relationships in your life."

It sounds like it makes sense — but every time I think about talking to my parents about this, I just want to purge. I tell Dr. Pardy that, even though I know it's going to go in my notes and might end up causing me to stay in here longer.

But surprisingly, she doesn't write on her clipboard or look disapproving. What she does is *smile* and nod her head like I've said something really profound.

"That's terrific, Janie," she says.

What?! Terrific that I want to *purge*? *Who the hell are you and what have you done with Dr. Pardy?*

It's like she reads my mind. "Not terrific that you feel like purging — but that you admit to it," she says. "So I'd like you to try and describe what emotions you're feeling right now, while you're sitting here thinking about purging."

I hate when she asks me to do this.

"The main emotion I have is that I want to purge," I say. "And frustration that I have to sit here and tell you about it and can't go off and do it, without some watchdog following me to make sure I don't."

"Okay, but let's try to get beneath that feeling of 'I want to purge.' If I were to say to you, 'Go ahead and purge, Janie,' what emotional payoff would you get from sticking your finger down your throat?"

"Lightness," Missy says.

"Emptiness," I say. "Like I don't have to feel anymore."

"It makes me feel calm," Callie adds. She gives me a pointed look. "The same way cutting does."

Ouch. I guess I was waiting for that. I didn't see Callie yesterday after I'd snitched on her to Nurse Kay. They moved me out of Callie's room and back into my old room with the new anorexic girl, which was a huge relief because I was afraid Callie would smother me with a pillow while I

204

slept or something. She completely ignored me at break-fast, like I was invisible, and I guess she's still pretty pissed. I can't say I blame her, either.

"So now we know the payoff," Dr. Pardy says. "What I'd like to explore are the feelings that are so heavy that Missy thinks she needs to purge to feel light, and so over-whelming that Janie wants to purge to empty herself of them, and so completely agitating that Callie feels the need to purge — and even cut herself — in order to feel calm again."

The silence is long and heavy.

"Don't all speak at once," Dr. P jokes. I didn't think she ever joked. I figure I owe it to her to take a stab at answering.

"It's hard to name just one feeling," I say. "Because usually when I want to purge it's like . . . this nameless feel-ing that's so big it doesn't have a name. . . ."

Suddenly, I picture Joe handing me the gloves and telling me to let loose on the punching bag.

"But I guess you could say anger is one of them."

Dr. Pardy smiles.

"Which makes perfect sense, given what you've been through," she says. "But it's important to recognize that anger and to let it out in a constructive way, rather than turning it inward on yourself."

I tell the group about Joe and the punching bag.

"You know what? I'm getting Joe to take me to the gym later," Callie says. "Then I can imagine *someone's* face on the bag."

It doesn't take a rocket scientist to know that *some-one's* identity.

"But isn't it more to do with the reason why we binge than the reason we purge?" Missy asks.

Dr. Pardy does the typical annoying shrink thing and answers Missy's question with a question.

"What *are* your reasons for bingeing, Missy?"

I think Missy was just *asking* the question rather than actually prepared to *answer* it.

"I don't know."

Dr. Pardy just looks at her.

"Well, I mean . . . I guess . . . sometimes it's just to try to fill the emptiness inside."

So Missy binges to fill the emptiness and I purge to get it back. I guess there's no "one size fits all" reason why we Barfers do what we do.

"One thing I can assure you is that food will only fill the emptiness temporarily," says Dr. Pardy. "What's more, since people tend to binge on sugary foods, the sugar surge and subsequent fall will exacerbate mood swings. But let's get back to Janie telling her parents."

How about let's not and say we did?

"I'd like to brainstorm ways other than purging that Janie can cope with her anxiety that her parents won't believe her, that they might not love her, and all the other 'what if' worries she's expressed."

"Exercise," says Royce. "When I'm stressed out, I go for a run or lift weights. It helps clear my head."

"Why doesn't it surprise me that you would suggest that?" Callie snorts.

"Royce is right," Tom pipes up. I can't believe he's sticking up for Royce after the guy's been such an asshole to him. Tom's obviously a much better person than I am. "Exercise does help with stress. Well, unless it's my dad who you're doing the exercise with . . . but that's another story." He gives a rueful laugh. "And for some of us, exercise is off-limits right now, so we've got to come up with other ways of dealing with stuff."

"I always see Janie scribbling in her notebook," Bethany says. "I mean, she's already on her second one. I've been here twice as long as she has and I've only filled up half of mine. Maybe she could write more about her feelings."

"Both good suggestions." Dr. Pardy asks, "Any other ideas?"

"My father's been in and out of AA," Callie says. "The few times that things actually went well, he called his sponsor when he felt like having a drink."

Wow. So her father's an alcoholic on top of everything else. I guess maybe it's not surprising that Callie's so mad at the world.

"That's another good strategy," Dr. Pardy says, "Speaking to someone else when you feel like bingeing or purging."

When no one else seems to be able to think of anything else, Dr. P turns to me.

"So, Janie, you've been given some great ideas of how you can try to deal with your emotions in more constructive ways than bingeing and purging. Do you feel any more equipped to have a dialogue with your parents?"

Not really. To be honest, I don't think I'll *ever* be equipped to have a dialogue with my parents.

"Uh . . . yeah, I guess."

"Well, I'll speak to your parents and try to set up a family meeting for tomorrow morning."

Tomorrow morning?! Why so soon? Can't she give me more time to figure this all out? But maybe she figures she'd better get me to strike while the iron is hot or something, to get it over with before I have a chance to think about it too much and chicken out.

My stomach churns and I want to purge more than ever. *Okay. Think, Janie! Exercise. Talk. Write.* As soon as group ends, I'm going to go beg Joe to take me to the gym.

CHAPTER FIFTEEN

August 6th

Steps one and two — Okay, I've been to the gym, beaten the punching bag to within an inch of its leather-bound life, and talked to Joe about how nervous I am about talking to my parents later and how just the thought of it makes me want to stick my fingers down my throat. Now it's time for step three — writing.

"What's the worst that could happen?" Joe asked me when I'd worked up a sweat.

"I don't know. I guess that they wouldn't believe me, or that they'd think I'm a slut or something and blame me for having sex with Matt in the first place."

"I'll tell you something that works for me," Joe said. "When I'm feeling anxious about a situation that could have multiple outcomes, I think of what the absolutely worst outcome could be — and I try to accept it. Once I do that, I'm not afraid of facing

209

the situation anymore, because in my mind I've already made peace with the worst thing that could possibly happen."

So that's what I'm trying to do here, before I meet with my parents and Dr. Pardy in half an hour. I'm trying to accept that my parents might well think I'm a slut and that it's my fault. Or that they just won't believe me at all, and they'll think it's all just something I made up so they aren't as mad at me about Jenny's wedding and the Xanax. But how do you go about accepting the possibility that your parents don't believe you when you tell them that something awful happened? Or if when you finally get up the courage to tell them, they think the worse of you for doing so?

I'm not sure I can accept them doing that. But I guess I can accept the fact that I'll be really sad — and probably, if I'm willing to admit it, really, really angry — if they do.

Well, here goes nothing . . .

My parents are doing their best Madame Tussauds imitation when I enter Dr. Pardy's office. I'm not exactly what you'd call relaxed myself, but at least I've prepared myself for feeling like crap if things go the way I expect them to — in other words, badly.

"I appreciate you coming to meet here on such short notice," Dr. Pardy tells my parents. "Janie has made quite a breakthrough, and I felt that it would help her to be able to discuss it with you sooner rather than later."

Later would be fine by me. No, let's get it over with.

"A breakthrough? Why, that's terrific, honey!" Mom says. "Does that mean Janie will be able to come home soon?"

Yes. Does it?

"Let's hold off on that discussion until after she's had a chance to speak with you," Dr. Pardy says. "Why don't you start, Janie?"

I would give anything — not kidding, anything — to be able to get my ass to a bathroom and purge right now, rather than having to start this discussion with my parents. But everyone is sitting there, looking at me expectantly.

So I launch in, looking at a spot on the wall in between my parents so that it looks like I'm looking at them but I don't actually have to see the expressions on their faces when I tell them about how I lost my virginity to the son of one of Dad's biggest clients in the aforementioned client's pool house.

I manage not to cry while I'm recounting what went down in the Lewis's cabana, but when it comes to the wedding . . . when I tell them about how it felt when I realized that what was so special for me was nothing to Matt, it brings back all of the agony I felt on that night, like I've picked the scab off of a really fresh and painful wound.

It's only when I finish speaking that I'm able to look directly at my parents. My mother is reaching for the box of tissues, tears running down her face. My father looks completely shell-shocked. Neither of them says anything, which freaks me out because I need to know what they're thinking.

"I always thought the Lewis kid was so polite and well-mannered," Dad says in a monotone. "Shows how much *I* know."

"Wh — why didn't you tell us, Janie?" Mom sniffs.

"Because . . . I was scared."

"Scared of what?" Mom asks. "Did that boy threaten you?"

It's like Mom can't bring herself to say Matt's name after hearing what happened. I know how she feels.

"No! I wasn't scared of him. I was scared of *you* . . . and Dad. Scared that you wouldn't believe me. Or that you'd be mad at me. Plus I was afraid because Mr. Lewis is Dad's client and all and . . ."

"But you're our *daughter*!" Mom says. "We *love* you."

"Not as much as Jenny," I blurt out before I can stop myself. "I'll never be as perfect as she is."

Then I hate myself for saying it.

"Jenny's not perfect," Mom says. "Neither is Harry. Neither am I, and neither is your father."

"Dad thinks she is. I'll never live up to Jenny in Dad's eyes."

"How can you think that, Pussycat?" Dad says. I'm shocked to see that his eyes are shining with tears. I don't think I've ever seen my father teary-eyed before, even at my grandmother's funeral.

"Well, because you're always telling me how I should be more like Jenny, how I should study hard like Jenny, so I can get into Yale like Jenny and marry a nice investment banker . . . just like Jenny," I tell him. "And you think what *Jenny* does has meaning and value, whereas you think the stuff that's important to *me*, like doing drama, isn't important."

"But your father is incredibly proud of you and your acting!" Mom says. "You should hear him bragging about you to all of our friends."

"Well, maybe you should try bragging about me to *me*," I tell Dad.

It's strange. At home, Dad is always the one doing the talking, who knows what to say, who takes charge of the situation. But here, he looks totally bewildered . . . like this is so out of what he would call his "areas of competence" that he's happy to let Mom wear the pants, so to speak.

"I'm sorry, Pussycat. Really I am," Dad says, wiping his eyes. "I guess your old dad might be good at managing money, but not so great at being a dad."

Hearing my normally totally confident and self-assured dad sounding so humble makes me start crying again, too.

"You *are* a good dad," I sob. "I just want to feel like you're as proud of me as you are of Jenny, that's all."

"Don't ever doubt that, honey," Dad says. "Don't ever doubt that. I guess I'll have to make an effort to tell you more, huh?"

Dr. Pardy has been silently watching and listening, but now she chimes in to our little family Sob Fest.

"I think the lesson here is how easy it is to hold on to misconceptions if there isn't good communication within a family," she says.

"I thought we *did* communicate," Mom says. "I guess I was wrong."

"You guys have been so wrapped up in the Wedding of the Century you haven't really been listening to a whole lot else."

"I'm sorry, sweetheart. I know things have been a bit crazy these last few months," Mom says.

"More than a bit."

Dad leans forward in his chair. "Honey, I wanted to give Jenny and Brad a good start to their life together." He takes out a monogrammed handkerchief from his suit pocket and blows his nose. "Just like someday, I hope to do the same thing for you."

I'm considering telling him that I plan to elope, when Dr. Pardy begins to speak.

"Let's talk a bit about what kind of support Janie will need when she is released from Golden Slopes," she says. "Because I think some family therapy would be helpful, on top of the need for Janie to find a good individual therapist."

"When can Janie come home?" Mom asks.

"I think if we can get the posthospitalization treatment plan in place, the day after tomorrow," Dr. Pardy says, smiling.

The day after tomorrow? I can't believe it — I thought I'd be stuck in here for eternity!

Dr. Pardy hands my mother a yellow pad so Mom can take notes about the things she needs to get sorted out before they'll let me out of here. They have to know that Mom's set up an appointment for me with a therapist within a week of my getting out of here, and that we've got some family counseling sessions on the calendar, too. I'm nervous about who my therapist will be — although I guess I didn't have a whole lot of choice about Dr. Pardy and she turned out to be okay. Now that I've learned how to spill my guts to a room full of virtual strangers, speaking to one person under shrink-patient privilege should be a cinch, right?

When the Things to Do Before Janie Is Sprung list is completed, Dad stands up and shakes Dr. Pardy by the hand.

"Thank you, Doctor. I have to tell you, I've been a lifelong skeptic about shrinks, but you seem to be the real deal, and I really appreciate what you've done to help our Janie."

"Believe me, Mr. Ryman, it's been my pleasure. Janie is a bright and insightful young lady, who has made tremendous progress while she's been here."

Mom hugs me.

"I can't wait to have my girl back home," she says. "We've missed you so much."

"What, even when I talk back and roll my eyes and tell you how you're ruining my life?"

"Even then," Mom says, her eyes filling up for what must be the zillionth time.

"Take care of yourself, Pussycat," Dad says. "And don't forget — your old dad loves you."

"I love you, too, Dad."

I know that in life these conversations don't happen all that often. So when one does — especially when you've been convinced that your parents are going to hate you when you tell them something and they tell you they love you instead — it feels pretty damn . . . special.

*It's weird, I've been dying to get out of this place
for every single minute of the almost three weeks
I've been in here . . . but now that it's actually going
to happen tomorrow, I'm scared. I don't know if I'm
ready to face life on the outside. What am I going
to say to people? I bet everyone in the whole world
knows about what happened at Jenny's wedding,
and that they're all going to think that I'm this
totally screwed-up freak. At least in here, everyone
else is a totally screwed-up freak, too. What if that
ends up being my identity for the rest of high
school — the girl who ended up in a mental hospital
after she completely lost it at her sister's wedding?
What if Matt Lewis tells everyone that I was a
virgin? What if he tells everyone that I'm easy?*

*As I write this, I feel my shoulders tensing up
and my jaw starting to clench and, if I'm willing to
admit this to myself, I'm feeling the urge to purge.
Strategies! Strategies!*

*Maybe I'll go talk to one of the nurses in a little
while. But first, I think of what Joe said to me in the
gym when I was freaking out about how my parents would react. So I try to think of the worst case
scenarios — the entire school knowing that I lost my
virginity to Matt Lewis in his parents' pool house,
and that I was stupid enough to think that it actually meant something to him, that I might end up
being known as "Crazy Janie" for the rest of my
days at Pine Ridge High, that other guys might*

think that because I gave it up to Matt Lewis, who I'd crushed on for four years, that I'm some kind of slut who will do it with anyone.

How do I accept it if those things really happen, because it would so totally and completely suck?

Then I think about my best friends, Kelsey and Danny. Will they stop being my friends just because I was stupid enough to believe in Matt Lewis, who Kelsey at least knows I've worshiped from afar for years? I don't think so. Will Danny hate me because I slept with Matt? Well, I'm pretty sure he and Nicole Hartman were doing it while they were dating last summer, and I sure as hell don't hate him.

Jenny and Brad, if they haven't forgiven me, at least don't completely hate me, and if they can still love me after what I did at their wedding, why should I care what an asshole like Matt Lewis says or does? And my parents, who I thought wouldn't believe me, who I thought would think it was all my fault, came through for me.

So while I'm not denying that it will completely suck if everyone is talking about me and thinks I'm this crazy, screwed-up chick, I know I'll live. What's more, I know I want to. I've got to remember to thank Harry for calling 911 when I get home.

CHAPTER SIXTEEN

August 9th

I'm FREE!!! It feels so good to be home, sleeping in my own bed. To be able to put a napkin in my lap while I eat dinner and to pick the cucumbers out of the salad. Best of all is being able to go to the bathroom without someone listening at the door — although Mom's been pretty vigilant about keeping an eye on me for at least half an hour after every meal, which is getting old fast, but I guess I understand why she's doing it, even though it's making me crazy. So to speak.

When I got home, I hugged Ringo, who was running around and barking with excitement. Then I hugged my brother, Harry, who put up with it for a moment, but then was like, "All right, jeez, enough of the mushy stuff!" But I didn't let him go right away — I looked him in the eye and said, "Thanks for calling 911, squirt."

"Yeah, whatever," was his sentimental reply. He can't help it really; he's just a twelve-year-old boy.

It was hard to leave my friends at Golden Slopes, though. I felt guilty that I was going to be buzzed out of the locked doors and they were still going to be stuck in that place.

I got people to write their e-mail addresses and IM screen names in the back of this journal. I wonder if we'll all keep in touch, or if once we get back to our "real" lives, we'll want to just forget about everything to do with what happened at Camp Golden Slopes. I hope not, because I want to know how things go with everyone. I worry that they're all going to be okay. I wonder how it'll be for Tom when he comes out to his friends at school. Will they be supportive or will they be assholes like his dad? I wonder if Dr. Pardy will ever be able to get to the bottom of what's up with Callie. I want Callie to be able to get through life, no matter how awful it is, without gouging herself. I want Tracey to figure out that there's more to her than wife and mother, to learn what makes her tick, and even more importantly, what makes her happy. I want Missy's mom to realize that the stepdad is a creep. I want Tinka to get well enough to finish at Harvard and Bethany to be able to eat peas instead of hiding them in her sock.

I often think about Helen. What makes the difference between ending up like her, dead, or being considered "cured" enough to leave Golden Slopes and get on with your life, like me? I think about what would have happened if Harry hadn't ignored my parents and called 911 when he did. Could I have died? As awful as I felt that morning, I know now that I'd rather be here than in a box in the ground like Helen.

The irony is that even though I'm alive and free, I'm afraid to leave the house. I feel like a turtle without its shell — naked and vulnerable. I'm afraid to go to Starbucks, I'm afraid to go to the beach, I'm afraid to go to the mall, I'm afraid to go anywhere in case I bump into anyone I know. Pathetic, isn't it?

Maybe I just need some time to heal, to lick my wounds — or maybe I'm just being a coward.

"C'mon, Janie," Kelsey pleads. "You can't keep hiding away in your house forever. Change into your bathing suit. I'm taking you to the beach."

"I can't go to the beach!" I wail. "We might . . . SEE people."

"That's the point, you doofus! School starts in two weeks. You're going to have to 'see people' then and you might as well get a bit of practice to ease into it slowly."

The thought of being around lots of people scares the hell out of me. I still feel so raw and exposed. But deep down I know that, as usual, Kelsey's right. Maybe I need to get this whole "being out there with other people" thing over with sooner rather than later.

So we get into Kelsey's car and drive to the beach.

I'm wearing an oversize T-shirt over my bathing suit, with no intention of taking it off, even to swim.

We spread our beach towels on an empty patch of sand.

"It's so hot and humid," Kelsey complains. "We need a celebratory ice cream — my treat. What do you want?"

I'm about to say "no, thanks," because of the fat and the calories, but then I remember something Dr. Pardy said about *acting opposite*; about how if my instinct is to do something that is part of my eating disordered behavior, I should consciously do the opposite. *What the hell*, I figure. *How many calories can there be in a Fudgsicle*?

Kelsey goes off to the concession stand in pursuit of ice cream, and I'm about to lie down in my jumbo T-shirt when I think *what the hell* again. I whip off the T-shirt and sprawl out on the towels.

It's bizarre. I'm lying on the beach wearing a bathing suit without a T-shirt for the first time in at least two years. For once in my life I feel entirely at home in my own skin, with no shame for how I look or who I am. I actually kind of . . . like . . . myself. How strange is that? I'm not thinking about flabby thighs or a fat ass or anything other than how warm and comforting the sand feels beneath my feet, and how the soft breeze lifts my hair back from my face, but miraculously, without making it look like the usual ball of frizz. The sun caresses my face gently, tenderly, like the hero in a movie right before he leans in to kiss the heroine. Gulls call to each other overhead, as children laugh and fight over shovels.

I open my eyes and look out across the sand to where the sun's rays have laid a blanket of diamonds on the water's surface. I wish I could scoop up those diamonds, one by one, to help me remember this feeling when the old insecurities creep back into my head, when I start hearing that bitchy, critical voice playing the same negative tapes in my head. To remind me that I am worthwhile and deserving of respect from myself and others. To remind me that I have a voice and I can use it. That even when I feel trapped and frustrated, there's always a choice — even if it isn't an easy or a pleasant one. Because *I'm* the director of *The Janie Ryman Story*, and whether it's a comedy or a tragedy is about where I choose to point the camera lens.

I close my eyes again, mentally collecting sun-diamond memories to store in my inner keepsake box, when I feel a shadow across my body, blocking out the sun.

"Hey, Janie. Long time no see."

I open my eyes and look up into the tanned face of Danny Epstein. "I've missed you," he says, looking for all the world like he's blushing under his tan — surely not because of *me*?

"I heard you were . . ." he pauses. "Away."

I feel my stomach clench and my first instinct is to reach for my T-shirt, to feel embarrassed and ashamed, to want to cover up my stomach and breasts and thighs and butt, all those parts of me that are so imperfect and unlovely. But then I reach out to the horizon with my hand and pluck another imaginary diamond off the water's surface. I remind myself that I'm more than a size of clothing or a number on a scale, and that I don't have to be perfect, I just have to be me, Janie Ryman, and if that's not good enough for people, then, as Missy would say, "Fuck 'em!"

"I was in the hospital," I say. "Getting treated for bulimia."

There. I've handed it to him to throw back in my face. I sit up and square my shoulders, bracing myself for the impact of rejection. But amazingly, it doesn't come.

"Do you mind if I sit down?" Danny asks.

"Uh, not at all," I say, scooching over to make room for him on my towel. He sits down, close enough that I can feel the warmth radiating from his skin, but not so close that I feel crowded and uncomfortable. His legs are muscular, covered with fine hair that's been bleached with the sun and a light dusting of sand.

"I heard that, too," he admits. "You know, it really surprised me because you're one of the most together girls I've ever met."

I burst out laughing. It's not like I'm being rude or anything, but I can't help seeing humor in the chasm between how Danny sees me and the walking disaster area that's been the real Janie Ryman.

"What?" he says. "What's so funny?"

"I just can't believe you think I'm together when I just got out of what is basically a mental hospital after swallowing a handful of Xanax."

My eyes drop from his face to stare at my toes, half buried in the sand. "Especially since . . . well, especially since the last time you saw me I was crying and covered in chocolate puke at Jenny's wedding. I mean seriously, dude, how much *less* together can a girl get?"

He puts his hand on my knee. Surprised, I turn to look

223

at him; his touch brings a mixture of shock and strangely . . . excitement. His eyes leave mine and he looks out over the horizon. "Janie, even crying hysterically and covered in puke while wearing what must be the most hideous bridesmaid dress in nuptial history . . ."

I laugh, because having been seen in public wearing that lemon-meringue bridesmaid's dress, which I was so sure Jenny and Clarissa chose just to spite me, seemed like such a huge trauma at the time, but now, in light of everything I've been through, it just seems so incredibly . . . minor.

"Well, despite all of those things — you know, the puke patterns actually *improved* that dress, which is saying something . . ."

"Despite all of those things *what*?"

"Despite all of those things, you are still one of the most beautiful and together girls I've ever met."

I must have been out in the sun for too long. Or maybe I've got water in my ears. Or sand in my brain. There's just no way in hell that I could have heard Danny correctly. Not a chance.

I turn to look at him, but he's still staring out at the horizon with the fixed intensity of a Secret Service agent.

"Say something," he says softly.

"Something."

The corner of his mouth turns up slightly, like he wants to smile but his face muscles are too tight to let him. He's still resolutely looking anywhere but at me.

"Something else, *you dork*!"

What can I say? What should I say? I feel a familiar wave of panic in my stomach. I don't want to blow this by saying the wrong thing. Danny has been my friend since what seems like forever, always funny, always teasing, always . . . there. Even when he's giving me a hard time about something, it's always been with this underpinning of . . . I don't know . . . kindness? Friendship? Maybe . . . love?

It's strange. I've always been attracted to the bad boys, who are good-looking, dangerous, out of reach. The guys who either look right through me, or just use me without even trying to know who I really am. The Matt Lewises of this world.

But Danny has always been different: trustworthy, safe, comfortable, but just not . . . exciting. Except now, I feel this current between us that is anything but boring. Maybe I've been guilty of looking right through Danny.

I decide to give him another gift of trust.

"That was the worst night of my life," I whisper. "I acted like a complete idiot. I upset Jenny on her wedding day, and all over that moron, Matt Lewis, who didn't deserve me anyway."

Danny finally pries his eyes from the horizon.

"I'll say. Anyway, don't be too hard on yourself, Janie," he says with a grin. "You know, even perfect, together girls like you are entitled to make a mistake once in a while."

I do what any self-respecting girl in my position would do. I punch him.

"OW!" he says, grabbing my hand and tickling my side where he knows I'm extra ticklish. All of a sudden we're giggling and wrestling like when we were in grade school, except this time when he finally leans across to pin me to the towel, we stop laughing. I gaze up into his eyes.

His mouth is a few inches away from mine when he says, "I wish, more than anything, that I'd punched Matt Lewis that night. It makes me crazy that he hurt you like that."

"Me, too," I whisper.

I think he's going to kiss me. I want him to kiss me. I'm scared to death of him kissing me.

"Hey, Danny! If I'd known you were coming, I'd have gotten three ice creams."

What do you know? I'm Saved by the Fudgsicle, and I'm not entirely sure I'm happy about it. But I guess it gives me a chance to get used to the idea of Danny Epstein as someone other than my childhood friend, as someone that I actually might want to *kiss*.

"Hey, Critelli! You'll just have to let me eat half of yours now, won't you?" Danny says.

"As if! If you think I'm sharing my Toasted Almond with anyone, you've got another thing coming, dude!"

"Girls. All they ever think about is food," Danny says.

I see Kelsey give him a dirty look and he cringes.

"I'm such a jerk. I'm sorry, Janie. I shouldn't joke about that."

I can tell I need to nip this in the bud.

"Well, yeah, you are a jerk...but seriously, guys, you've got to stop tiptoeing around me. Around every mention of food. I'm not going to run and stick my finger down my throat just because you crack a joke."

They exchange glances, seeking nonverbal opinions

if they should take my word on this. I take a bite of my Fudgsicle. I'm starting to get mad.

"See. I can even eat ice cream. You can make me sit here for half an hour afterward if you want just to check up on me. Kelsey can accompany me to the john to make sure I don't purge, if you're that worried. Sorry, Danny, boys not allowed."

The expression of shock on both of their faces is comical. I'm about to reach for my cell phone to snap a picture of them, mouths open, eyes wide. I guess people aren't used to me opening my mouth to speak up when I'm not on stage in a play using other people's words. But having done it, I feel brave, reckless almost. Maybe Dr. Pardy was right about this "using your voice" business. I reach my hand up to Danny's chin and gently push his jaw closed.

"You'd better shut your mouth, Epstein, or you'll be catching flies in there," I say.

I take a bite of Fudgsicle and hand the rest to Danny.

"I need to take a swim," I say, and feeling lighter and happier than I have felt in years, I run down to the water and dive in.

Floating on my back, eyes closed, I feel at peace with myself and the world, and I'm able to really "live in the moment," as Ali would say. A few minutes later I hear splashes and Danny and Kelsey are there, floating beside me.

I know I'll never be completely cured, because being bulimic isn't like being an alcoholic. I can't say, "I'll never eat again," because then I'd be anorexic and risk ending up like Helen. I know I have to face my "enemy," food, at least three times a day every day for the rest of my life. But lying here in the water, the sun shining on my face with my best friends in the outside world by my side, and the supportive voices of my Golden Slopes friends in my head instead of that self-critical inner voice, I know I can do this. Because once you've faced down a plate of cucumbers and won, anything is possible.

ACKNOWLEDGMENTS

Ellen Wittlinger is this book's fairy godmother. She wove her magic during a workshop on inspiration at the 2006 Kindling Words retreat in Vermont. Thanks to all KW participants that year, particularly Nancy Werlin, Sarah Aronson, Elise Broach, and Chris Tebbetts, for helping me to reconnect with my writing process.

Thanks to Robin Friedman for the title.

My agent, Jodi Reamer, deserves a medal.

Bill Buschel, Gay Morris, Susan Warner, Steve Fondiller, Alan Shulman, and the amazing Diana Klemin critiqued this work with humor and love.

Jen Rees and David Levithan are editors who make revising fun.

Thanks to my family, Susan and Stanley Darer, John Darer, Anne Darer and Mark Davis, Dylan and Daniel Davis, and Lindsay Cullingford (a.k.a. "Mary Poppins") for their love and support.

Hank Eskin keeps me grounded and knows when to provide chocolate.

My children, Joshua and Amie, give my life meaning

in so many wonderful ways and allow me to embarrass them by the mere fact of my existence. I love you.

Lastly, to all the patients and professionals I encountered in my journey to recovery . . . thank you. I've learned so much from each and every one of you.

EATING DISORDER RESOURCES

If you think you have a problem with body image or food, remember — you're not alone. The best thing you can do is to seek help, even though the insidious voice of your eating disorder will try to talk you out of it. Be warned that when you do seek help, you might not always get the best response. When I finally got up the courage to admit to my doctor that I was bulimic, the first thing he said to me was, "I suppose telling you to stop won't do any good." I felt like saying, "Well, DUH! If I could just stop, I wouldn't be here asking you for help, would I?" But don't give up! I thank heaven for the Internet, where I was able to find more supportive voices. And fortunately, a year or so later, I found The Wilkins Center and Dr. Diane Mickley, a doctor with an infinitely more constructive approach. That made all the difference for my recovery.

WEB SITES

National Eating Disorders Association
www.edap.org
Offers a wealth of resources, including a toll-free treatment referral help line (1-800-931-2237) and curricula for teaching healthy body image to school-age children. NEDA also sponsors National Eating Disorder Awareness Week.

Bulimia Nervosa Resource Guide
www.bulimiaguide.org
From the ECRI Institute, a comprehensive, free resource on bulimia nervosa available for download in PDF format.

Something Fishy
www.something-fishy.org
A safe environment to support recovery. Includes information and online message boards to help connect people suffering from eating disorders.

Academy for Eating Disorders
http://aedweb.org
A global organization for eating disorder professionals and a wonderful source for all the latest research in the field.

ANAD
(National Association of Anorexia Nervosa and Associated Eating Disorders)

In addition to great information, ANAD offers speakers for schools and has links to clinics and therapists that specialize in the treatment of eating disorders.

BOOKS

The Body Project: An Intimate History of American Girls by Joan Jacobs Brumberg. Tracks how the emphasis has changed from developing a girl's character to focusing on her looks, over the course of the last century.

Life Without Ed: How One Woman Declared Independence from Her Eating Disorder and How You Can Too by Jenni Schaefer with Thom Rutledge. Humorous and powerful, Schaefer learns to visualize her eating disorder as "Ed," a unique personality separate from her own — and an abusive one at that — and gains the strength to "divorce" the rotten, no-good scoundrel.

The Body Betrayed: A Deeper Understanding of Women, Eating Disorders, and Treatment by Kathryn J. Zerbe, MD. An intelligent, sensitively written book about the causes of eating disorders.

<gaining> the truth about life after eating disorders by Aimee Liu. A realistic yet ultimately hopeful book about life in recovery.

101 Ways to Help Your Daughter Love Her Body by Brenda Lane Richardson and Elane Rehr. This book has practical strategies for parents to try to counter-act the negative messages that bombard girls on a daily basis.

In addition, Gurze Books (http://www.gurze.com) specializes in books, videos, and periodicals about eating disorders, and their site is worth checking out.

TREATMENT

The Wilkins Center for Eating Disorders
http://wilkinscenter.com
An outpatient facility in Greenwich, CT, founded by the truly inspirational Dr. Diane Mickley.

Eating Disorder Referral and Information Center
www.edreferral.com
Offers referrals to eating disorder specialists and treatment facilities on a state-by-state basis.